ET TU, BABE

ET TU, BABE

MARK LEYNER

HARMONY BOOKS • NEW YORK

Published by Harmony Books, a division of Crown Publishers, Inc., 201 East 50th Street, New York, New York 10022.

Member of the Crown Publishing Group.

Random House, Inc. New York, Toronto, London, Sydney, Auckland

HARMONY and colophon are trademarks of Crown Publishers, Inc.

Manufactured in the United States of America

Book Design by Anne Scatto

Library of Congress Cataloging-in-Publication Data

Leyner, Mark.
Et tu, babe / Mark Leyner. — 1st ed.
p.   cm.
I. Title.
PS3562.E99E85   1992   92-8020
813'.54—dc20   CIP

ISBN 0-517-58335-6

10   9   8   7   6   5   4   3   2   1

First Edition

TO MICHAEL PIETSCH,
THE MONSTER MAKER

PREFACE

June 6, 1993
Hoboken

Dear Peter Guzzardi,

As you know, I am not your average author. I dress like an off-duty cop: leather blazer, silk turtleneck, tight sharply creased slacks, Italian loafers, pinky-ring. I drive a candy-apple red Jaguar with a loaded 9-mm semiautomatic pistol in the glove compartment. When I walk into a party I'm like this: my head is bobbing to music that only exists in my mind. For our seventh anniversary, I gave my wife, Arleen Portada, a rotating diamond-impregnated drill bit—the kind that German and Russian geologists use in their deep drilling programs—programs that produce ultradeep holes with depths of up to 15 kilometers. But that's just the kind of guy I am. Dynamic. Robust. No nonsense. A steak and chops man. Double scotch rocks. A man who makes things happen. Big hairy hands. A powerful fist that comes down on a conference table with peremptory authority. Then there's stunning Arleen Portada. Mystic. Sensualist. Why she covered with centipede stings?

3

If you spent all day on a sun-baked prairie wearing a sizzling orange minidress supervising a platoon of beefy workmen as they paint immense grain silos vibrant yellow and fuchsia, you'd be covered with centipede stings, too.

My whole life has been one long ultraviolent hyperkinetic nightmare. But yes, I am an author. (And a dog trainer—Peter, I taught my puppy Carmella to drink scalding hot black coffee out of her bowl on the floor!) The other day, I imagined that it was the year 2187—a dozen people were gathered at the grave site of porn star John Holmes to commemorate the 200th anniversary of his death. Well, Peter, I want to be remembered by more people than that. I don't know . . . perhaps that's why I write.

The unwashed armpits of the most beautiful women in the world . . . a urinal with chunks of fresh watermelon in it . . . a retarded guy whining "Eddie, Eddie, get me an Ovaltine"— almost anything inspires me. Immediately after finishing *MY COUSIN, MY GASTROENTEROLOGIST,* I outlined a new book about people with trichotillomania—people who compulsively pull out their hair. There are 2 million to 4 million Americans who have trichotillomania. That's a lot of books! (That's a lot of hair, too!) I abandoned that idea though—that's not the kind of book that Harmony wants from a Mark Leyner, right? Well, I'm confident that, after perusing the following excerpts, you'll agree that the novel I hereby propose is indeed the kind of book that Harmony wants from a Mark Leyner.

ET TU, BABE—a master jam of relentless humor and indeterminate trajectories—teeming with creatures and the burlesque of their virulent lives—will undoubtedly be, page by page and line by line, the most entertaining book that Harmony has ever published.

4

ET TU, BABE

The four-foot hermaphroditic organism from a distant solar system twitched in my arms as I soul-kissed it. The laboratory director would have killed me if he'd known that I'd snuck into the Galactic Lifeform Chamber with a bottle of wine, a cassette player, and an eclectic selection of tapes (Felix Mendelssohn, Steppenwolf, Barbara Mandrell) for a clandestine tryst with the cylindrical being whom the lab technicians had christened "Kitty Lafontaine." I pipetted a few drops of 1982 Napa Valley Zinfandel into its alimentary aperture. Its synesthetic sensory apparatus was distributed evenly across the entirety of its shiny outer sheath so it could see, hear, smell, touch, precognize, etc., from any point on its body. To say that holding Kitty Lafontaine in my arms was like nestling a large holiday beef log from Hickory Farms would certainly not convey the spine-tingling xenophilic libidinous awe I felt, but it would accurately convey the shape, mass, and weight of this fascinating creature who would irrevocably change all our lives that summer.

Dear Science Editor of the *Times,*

Frequently the counterman at a sandwich shop will ask "Do you want everything on it?" Well, what if you had a sandwich with literally "everything" on it? In other words, how large a sandwich roll would you need to accommodate all matter in the universe? And, as a corollary, imagine an inconceivably immense being capable of eating this almost infinitely capacious submarine sandwich. If this colossal creature began eating at the instant of the Big Bang, by what century would he be able to consume, digest, metabolize, and excrete the hypothetical hoagie? And would not this meal, by its very nature, exhaust time itself?

Dear Editors at *Swank,*

Your article on the sensitive areolas of large-breasted women was excellent. Also, thanks for the recipe for paella valenciana that you published in the October *Swank*. I'm no gourmet chef, but I made the dish for my girlfriend and after dinner she couldn't keep her prosthetic hands off my veiny nine-inch chorizo.

I had once intended to write an entire novel while having to urinate very badly. I wanted to see how that need affected the style and tempo of my work. I had found, for instance, that when I'm writing about a character who's in a Ph.D. program and I don't have to urinate badly, I'll have him do a regular three- or four-year program. But if I'm writing a novel and I have to urinate very very badly, then I'll push the character through an accelerated Ph.D. program in perhaps only two years, maybe even a year.

In 1987, I enrolled in a 12-step program for people who pistol-whip their tailors. First I had to admit to myself that pistol-whipping my tailor was, in fact, a problem. Today I take life one day at a time. Each day that passes without my having pistol-whipped my tailor is a victory . . . a solid step toward recovery.

-Do you believe in God?

-Yes, sir.

-Do you believe in an anthropomorphic, vengeful, capricious God who can look down on one man and give him fabulous riches and look down on another and say "you're history" and give him a cerebral hemorrhage?

-Yes, sir.

-You may take the stand. What is your full name?

-I am General Ramon Humberto Regaldo Rosa Cordoba Lopez.

-General Lopez, you are descended from a very illustrious family, is that not true?

-Yes, sir. My great-great-great-great-grandfather was a nobleman in Spain in the fifteenth century and it was he who first discovered that the atomized saliva of hunchbacks enhances the growth of flowers. He, in fact, retained a large staff of hunchbacks to sneeze on his tulips.

-General, are those your real nails?

-Sir?

-Are those your real fingernails?

-Yes, sir.

-General, you are a fucking liar!

-Objection, Your Honor!

-Your Honor, I can see, defense counsel can see, and the ladies and gentlemen of the jury can see that the General is wearing Lee Press-On Nails.

-Objection overruled. Continue.

-General, under direct examination you were asked to describe events that took place on the morning of April 26, 1987. You testified, and I quote: "I was a short thickset man with a fleshy, brutal face. I felt bad. I had been drinking heavily the previous night and the heat bothered me. My wife was sleeping. 'Wake up, stupid,' I snarled. I shook her and I kissed her savagely. 'You stink,' she sneered. 'Your breath smells like the steam that rises off fresh vomit.' I jabbed a syringe full of methamphetamine into her ass, which was covered with boils the size of potato pancakes." Is that still an accurate account to the best of your knowledge?

-Yes, sir.

-General, it strikes me as exceedingly odd that, asked to describe a particular morning on a particular day, you would say, "I was a short, thickset man with a fleshy, brutal face." Are we to understand by this that you were a short, thickset man with a fleshy, brutal face only on April 26, 1987?

-Objection, Your Honor. This kind of semantic nitpicking is an obvious form of harassment. The district attorney knows full well that the General was a short, thickset man with a fleshy, brutal face prior to April 26, 1987, that he was a short, thickset man with a fleshy, brutal face during April 26, 1987, and that he continues to be a short, thickset man with a fleshy, brutal face subsequent to April 26, 1987.

-Sustained.

-General, that afternoon, did you receive a call at the office from your wife?

-Yes, sir.

-What did she say?

-She said that she thought she'd been on her liquid formula diet long enough . . . that she was so light that the static electricity from the television set was pulling her across the floor toward the screen.

-And she called one more time later that afternoon?

-Yes, sir.

-And what did she say?

-She said that she didn't have much time to talk, that she was tied to the railroad tracks and the Bullet Train was coming.

-And that was the last time you ever spoke to her?

-Yes, sir.

-General, one final question. Do you have any tattoos?
-Yes, sir.
-On what part of your body and of what?
-I have $E = nhf$ (Max Planck's formula for the energy in radiation) tattooed on my penile glans.
-General, you are a pathological fucking liar!!
-Objection!!
-Overruled.
-General, I'd like you to look at your penile glans and read to the court what's tattooed on it.
-It says: $d = 16t^2$.
-Not $E = nhf$?
-No, sir.
-And what's the significance of $d = 16t^2$?
-It's Galileo's formula for the distance an object falls from its starting point as time elapses from the instant it's dropped.
-Your Honor, I have no further questions.
-General Lopez, you may step down.

The giant awoke, got high on drugs, masturbated, and then went into town to forage for a human-flesh breakfast. He stopped at an intersection where his eye was caught by the puffy orange Day-Glo parka of a postmenopausal crossing guard. He knelt down and plucked up the screaming crossing guard in his fingers and dropped her into a gunnysack slung across his back. He surveyed the town until he discerned the bright orange regalia of another prey whom he captured and then on to the next intersection and then on to the next and the next and the next until his gunnysack was filled with squirming crossing guards. He returned home and laid the gunnysack on the counter. He urinated and then he put some music on the stereo; it was a kind of music I'd never heard before—a single high-pitched oscillating tone.

The giant *peeled* the crossing guards. After his breakfast, the floor was littered with puffy orange Day-Glo parkas.

Why crossing guards? Japanese scientists speculate that their conspicuous puffy orange Day-Glo parkas make them particularly attractive prey. Why postmenopausal women? Japanese scientists point to reduced estrogen levels. They think that estrogen is bitter to the tongue of the giant and that he simply finds the low-estrogen women tastier. But there's an even more intriguing explanation. Estrogen deficiencies in postmenopausal women cause osteoporosis, which is characterized by brittle bones. In other words, postmenopausal women are crunchier.

Well, Peter, how does that sound to you? I'm ready for it, babe—I'm massaging IQ-enhancing balm into my temples and I'm loading up on Winstrol, the steroid that got sprinter Ben Johnson disqualified from the 1988 Olympic Games in Seoul.

It's a forty-minute hydrofoil ride from Hong Kong to Macao. Look out toward the horizon. There's big Arleen rising up out of the water. Her white gown is fluttering violently in the wind, her lace veil is congested with sea spume. Isn't she beautiful? Isn't she just fucking absolutely beautiful?

Oh, one last question, Peter. My agent has a supernumerary nipple below and slightly medial to her right breast. The nipple produces approximately one watt of heat, about the same as that given off by a miniature Christmas tree bulb. Is this a standard energy output?

Yours very truly,

Mark Leyner

CHAPTER ONE

Q: If you could offer the young people of today one piece of advice, what would it be?

A: When I was eight, I was sent to live on the melon farm of an uncle . . .

When I was eight, I was sent to live on the melon farm of an uncle—a sixth-grade dropout who attributed his IQ of 70 to sniffing gasoline and glue from the age of five, and whose manner of compulsively clawing at the skin behind his neck was a characteristic sign of amphetamine toxicity. One morning he served me a cereal that consisted of sweetened corn puffs and marshmallow, hook-nosed, bearded "Jews." I asked him never to serve that cereal to me again. The next morning, he set a heaping bowl of the same cereal on my place mat. I killed him with a 12-gauge shotgun blast before lunch. That night I buried him in the cyclone cellar. I stole his pickup truck and drove out to a huge diesel-run electric turbine plant near the outskirts of the city and I had my first sexual experience. Afterward, I lit a cigarette and looked up into the sky—there was God, wearing a pink polo shirt, khaki pants, and brown Top-Siders with no socks, his blond hair blowing in the powerful wind of charged particles and intense ultraviolet radiation from the galactic center. I hated him. And he hated me.

I have spent the majority of my 36 years in orphanages, reformatories, prisons, and mental institutions. I had four oboe teachers and each one fell into an irrigation sluice and drowned. I'd tried explaining to my social workers that I hated double-reed mouthpieces. I pleaded with them not to make me take lessons on any instrument in the oboe family, which also includes the English horn, the bassoon, and the double bassoon. But nobody listened.

I hated the other children. Especially the ones whose parents could afford to provide proper orthodontic care. I had to gnaw constantly. My incisors grew four to five inches a year: if I'd stopped gnawing, my lower incisors would have eventually grown until they pushed up into my brain, killing me. Over the years, I was treated for a slew of psychiatric and behavioral problems: dyslexia, depression, excessive anxiety, obsessive-compulsive disorder, alcoholism, illicit drug abuse, obesity, eating disorders, exhibitionism, persistent aggressive and violent behavior, and hyperactivity combined with severe attention deficits. Yet there was a voice within me that said: Someday you will be considered the most intense and, in a certain sense, the most significant young prose writer in America. And I listened.

Today I live in a lemon-yellow stucco mansion with sweeping views of the bay. Each morning, I nibble iced raw turtle eggs and chocolate-dipped strawberries in a garden ablaze with hibiscus and bougainvillea—a far cry from the anti-Semitic breakfast cereal forced upon me by my half-witted uncle on his squalid melon farm.

My advice to the young people of today? I'm tempted to say: Surround yourself with flunkies and yes-men and have naked slaves, perfumed with musk, fan you with plastic fronds as you write. Because that's what's worked for me. But what does history teach us?

The 83rd President of the United States, Hallux Valgus, had no mouth or gastrointestinal tract. How did this Christian Scientist who refused intravenous nourishment survive? Only during the autopsy following President Valgus's assassination were scientists given the opportunity to solve this riddle. After painstaking dissection and analysis, pathologists found that Valgus was nourished from within by symbiotic bacteria. Their research revealed that the "tissue" of his trophosome, a large body structure which comprised half of Valgus's torso and which Valgus kept concealed beneath his ubiquitous spandex unitard, was composed of closely packed bacteria—over 100 billion per ounce of tissue. They found that his blood, deep red from a rich supply of hemoglobin, absorbed oxygen, carbon dioxide, and sulfur dioxide from the polluted atmosphere and transported it to the trophosome. Thus ensured a rich supply of chemical resources, the bacteria living inside Valgus produced carbohydrates and proteins, which Valgus then metabolized. Hallux Valgus, the 83rd President of the United States. The first occupant of the Oval Office to depend on symbiotic chemoautotrophic bacteria living within him. (His long and detailed *Memoirs* provide a unique picture of the personalities and politics of his times.)

Be petulant, narcissistic, and charismatic. That's what President Valgus would have exhorted today's young men and women, had not a hit-squad of gnat-sized robots filed stealthily into his ear and mined his brain with plastic explosive. And love. Love with extreme lucidity and barbaric ferocity. One of my foster mothers couldn't wait to shove me onto the school bus each morning so that she could get inside, doff her frowzy terry cloth robe and greasy housedress, squeeze into her edible lingerie, and await the arrival of the electrician, plumber, UPS delivery man, cable TV installer, exterminator—whichever beefy workman was fortunate enough to ring the doorbell first. That's not what I mean by "love." When I use the word *love,* I'm thinking about the witty, urbane, wasp-waisted Arleen Portada.

They were the heady, idealistic days of the early Valgus administration. Congress had just officially designated Bernard Herrmann's shrieking score for strings composed for the shower murder scene in *Psycho* as the national anthem. The Look that year was "postcoital"—tousled hair, runny mascara, smeared lipstick. Scientists working on the Human Genome Initiative announced identification of the specific gene that not only predisposes a person to take dancing lessons, but that actually determines his or her dance predilection: ballet, jazz, tap, or ballroom. It had been an exceptionally rainy spring, and indeed on the day we met, the sun was out for the first time in weeks . . .

I was climbing trees that afternoon and Arleen happened to be below stalking live subjects for a research project she was doing as part of her MSW program at Fordham University. She shot me with air-rifle darts full of tranquilizer. I lost muscle control gradually—one hand missing its grip, then the other—and fell into a net Arleen held outspread below. She carried me tenderly back to the lab for processing and measurements: total length, arm length, chest diameter, testicle length and width. "Look at the lunch-pack on this guy," she said, appreciating my scrotum. I hadn't really been planning to "get involved," but how could I resist the subtle, sophisticated blandishments of this young and beautiful psychotherapist?

Winning your place in the hierarchy is a basic part of primate life and each day is a savage, pitiless battle for dominance—so don't expect everyone to like you. Today I *am* the most intense, and in a certain sense, the most significant young prose writer in America. And I have the body of a grotesquely swollen steroid freak. Yet, I have many enemies. And these enemies will hurt me, unless I hurt them first, ergo the punji sticks and claymore mines that riddle the grounds surrounding my headquarters. Ergo my phalanx of bodyguards: seven formerly frail, arthritic nonagenarian widows with heart disease selected from a nearby nursing home. Arleen and I took them in, treated them as members of our own family, administered large doses of synthetic human growth hormone and testosterone to each woman, and replaced her atrophied musculature with powerful artificial muscles made out of polymer gels that contract when electricity is applied and expand when the current is turned off. Do you want to see carnage unparalleled in the annals of internecine strife? Try laying a finger on me, Arleen, my dog Carmella, or one of my fans.

I had a friend from my high school wrestling team named Jorge. After graduation and for the entirety of his adult life, Jorge worked on a huge ant farm in southern New Jersey. Every morning Jorge would get into his car and drive to the ant farm. But one morning Jorge got into his car and he didn't drive to the ant farm—he selected suicide-exalting heavy metal music from among the cassettes in his glove compartment, and he turned the volume up full blast, and he headed north on the New Jersey Turnpike. After traveling for some 90 minutes, and having reached an area within a mile's proximity of Newark Airport, he exited the highway and pulled into a desolate industrial dump. He got out of the car, opened the trunk, and removed a shoulder-held Stinger antiaircraft missile launcher. And he proceeded to blow a Federal Express jet en route from Chicago out of the sky as it made its final descent. Miraculously, the crew was able to eject from the plummeting aircraft and parachute to safety. But the plane's entire cargo of overnight letters and parcels was destroyed. I visited Jorge on death row.

"How could you do it?" I asked.

"Every day of my life I went in to that goddamn ant farm. Every single day. And every single day it was the same goddamn routine—they'd feed me steak or chopped meat which I'd digest, and then they'd force me to regurgitate to feed the queen and her larvae. Day after day after day, year after year . . . I just couldn't take it anymore. I just couldn't. . . ."

He collapsed on the floor. I knelt down to help him, but he waved me away.

"There's nothing you can do. I've taken a massive dose of Bromadiallone—a powerful anticoagulant. In a minute I'm going to die of internal hemorrhaging. But please . . . there's one thing I want to tell the young people of today. If you . . ."

He began to lose consciousness. I shook him and wet his lips with a couple of drops of Gatorade.

"If you what, babe?"

"If you . . . if you squander your precious beautiful days on meaningless labor whose"—he coughed up blood—"whose ultimate purpose is to further enrich the ruling elite or solidify the hegemony of the state . . . you're a sucker."

His eyes rolled back in his head. I shook him furiously and threw the rest of my Gatorade in his face. But it was too late. He was gone.

CHAPTER TWO

First Fisherman [stammering]: Could you . . . uh . . . please . . .
[He hands the fish hook and worm to the Second Fisherman.] I
can't . . . I knew him . . . way back . . . high school . . . I just
can't . . . I can't bring myself to hook him . . .
Second Fisherman: You knew this worm?
First Fisherman: He was my . . . well, I was his . . . I . . . I knew
him . . . yes . . .
Second Fisherman: This particular worm?
First Fisherman: I knew the worm, OK? I can't hook him, all right?
No way . . . can't hook him. [He looks at worm.] I can't hook
you . . . no way I could hook you, man.
[Worm manages a weak smile.]
Second Fisherman: You want me to hook him?
First Fisherman: Please!

The trail of lavender azalea blossoms leads to the stadium, to the
locker room. Faces are almost unrecognizable in the heavy fog of
aerosol deodorant and jock-itch powder. Some of the strongest men
can barely move, encumbered by their massive plated stegosaurian
tails, which leave long trails of cheesy sebaceous excretion. The
strongest man of all, who wears a combination lock through a hole
in his nose, empties a box of Good & Plenty into the whirlpool. The
Second Fisherman walks to the whirlpool and, leaning over the edge,
stares into the gurgling vortex of pink and white.

21

The two scenes you have just seen, both from the 1979 film *Let's Not and Say We Did,* helped make Iron Man Wang—who played the role of the Second Fisherman—one of Hong Kong's most popular screen stars. Evincing a taut sexuality, high-wire anxiety, and vulnerable fair-haired eccentricity, Iron Man Wang is today attempting to parlay these attributes into political capital as he launches his campaign to become Hong Kong's Administrative Prefect. Across the street, there's a huge photograph of his face, emblazoned with the caption: "I'm Iron Man Wang, how are you this evening?"

I'm inside the King Fok Club—a Hong Kong mah-jongg parlor and lounge frequented by drug couriers, numbers runners, transsexual prostitutes, and off-duty cops. The bandstand is a green blur of jade drumsticks as the topless all-girl trio sweats through an aerobic repertoire of Buddy Rich covers. I'm dancing with Antoinette, who's so gorgeous it's hard to believe she was a man once—not only a man, but a Golden Gloves middleweight champion and then the head of a teamsters local that was considered the roughest on the East Coast, but let me tell you, she is absolutely ooh-la-la. I guess no matter how many pugs he KO'd in the ring and no matter how many scabs and union dissidents he savaged with his brass knuckles, there was always a beautiful woman struggling to emerge. Compliments to the surgeon, he sculpted a real Venus de Milo. I inhale her wicked perfume as we waltz, large pimples on her back spelling "Vote for Iron Man Wang" in Braille.

The band finishes its set, I bid Antoinette *bon soir* and *kung hei fat choy* after politely declining an hour of "infernal ecstasies," she vanishes into the smoke, and I return to the bar and order the house special, something called a Stinky Pinky: two parts gin, one part strawberry schnapps, one part O-amino acetomphenome, which is the primary odor component of extract from the anal sac of a Japanese weasel. Some people hate Stinky Pinkies, I think they're yummy, and I'm draining my sixth when there's a loud commotion outside—so I run out and there lying in the middle of the street is Antoinette. She's dying. But something quite extraordinary is happening in extremis. As she dies, she is gradually resuming masculine form. Whiskers sprout from her cheeks and chin. Her Adam's apple protrudes from her throat. Her breasts shrivel, and her chest, now broad and muscular, becomes matted with black curly hair. Her hips and buttocks shrink and a large penis rises from beneath her Lurex skirt, stiffening in the cool Hong Kong night.

Now, I'm a writer, but I've always fancied myself something of an amateur forensic pathologist. My favorite show—as Arleen will certainly corroborate—is "Quincy, M.E." So whenever I run across a corpse, I try to take advantage of the opportunity to do a quick autopsy. I kneel down beside Antoinette and get to work. "Does anyone have a tape recorder?" I ask the crowd. Silly question, this is Hong Kong—a dozen state-of-the-art, micro-format, voice-activated, digital audiocassette recorders with Dolby noise reduction are immediately proffered. I grab one and begin to dictate: "The decedent died as a result of craniocerebral trauma (skull fractures, subfrontal and temporal bone contusions, and an organizing subdural hematoma). Observation of brain tissue indicates that the decedent suffered from incipient cerebral sclerosis—an actual hardening and shrinking of the cerebral mass, a condition that in its advanced form would have reduced the size of the decedent's brain to that of a peach pit. Other significant postmortem findings include multiple round, depressed skin ulcers in various stages of healing on the lower abdominal wall, thighs, and left elbow consistent with "skin-popping scars" of chronic subcutaneous narcotism." I eject the cassette, return the recorder, and judging the proximity of the police by the rising volume of their sirens, decide that it's time for me to say good-bye to the King Fok Club and good-bye to Hong Kong for now. I hail a rickshaw and we sprint toward Kai Tak Airport.

It'll be a long flight home, but even as we prepare to take off,

I already perceive the geographical and cultural disjunction. I write on a napkin: "I feel like a seed in the digestive tract of a bird, being transported thousands of miles from one habitat to another." I sign the napkin and ask the stewardess to give it to the pilot. Fortunately, I'm seated next to a fascinating passenger. She's Flo, a chimpanzee selected by Jane Goodall from among chimps at Tanzania's Gombe National Park, who was taught a sign language vocabulary of over 2,000 words. Flo often appears on MacNeil-Lehrer, "Nightline" with Ted Koppel, and CNN, participating in panel discussions on animal rights, the use of animals in medical research and cosmetics testing, etc. Luckily I learned sign language when I dated the Academy Award–winning deaf actress Marlee Matlin when I lived in L.A., so communicating with Flo is no problem. I learn that she's flying to the States to "speak" at a demonstration against a new product that's been introduced by Burger Hut called Rhesus Pieces: bite-size chunks of rhesus monkey coated in granola and deep-fried.

Even though it's quite expensive, I splurge and take the Glass-bottom Bus from Newark Airport back to headquarters. Upon my return, I find Arleen in bed, fast asleep, a book called *Object Relations Group Psychotherapy* open across her softly rising bosom. I kiss her warm lips and whisper, "I love you." Carmella is also asleep. I lift her ear flap and whisper, "I had a great time in Hong Kong—I'll tell you about it tomorrow. Good night, babe," I say, stroking her. The first autumn night of the year . . . I fall asleep with a feeling of profound contentment. How strange that I'll abruptly awaken in the middle of the night and clamber like a zombie to the roof—my eyes blazing in the darkness like the cigarette I smoke so rabidly!

It was determined at an October 17th meeting—attended by my literary agent Binky Urban, editor Peter Guzzardi, publicist Susan Magrino, and lecture agent George Greenfield—that I disguise my appearance before entering the Hyatt Self-Surgery Clinic in New Brunswick, New Jersey. Although the dimpled, clean-shaven face framed by blond-flecked chestnut tresses combed back into an undulating pompadour had become an instant icon to millions of fans who clipped photos from the pages of *Rolling Stone, Creem,* the *New York Times,* and the *Asbury Park Press* and pasted them to dormitory walls and three-ring binders, sometime in early November, a makeup artist was summoned to Team Leyner headquarters and instructed to execute a temporary new Look. The Look was Hezbollah—Party of God— closely cropped black hair, black beard, white button-down shirt, black pants.

The Hyatt Self-Surgery Clinic? Self-surgery clinics were the medical equivalent of U-Hauls or rental rug shampooers. Clinics provided a private operating room, instruments, monitoring devices, drugs, and instructional videocassettes for any procedure that could be performed solo, under local anesthetic, on any part of your anatomy that you could reach easily with *both* hands. As I pulled into the parking lot of the recently renovated Hyatt, I realized that I'd left my copy of Edmund Spenser's *The Faerie Queene* in the Mercury Capri XR2 that I'd test-driven for *Gentleman's Quarterly.* All my notes on the 132-hp turbocharged roadster were scrawled in the margins of the Elizabethan poet's magnum opus. I called Casale Lincoln Mercury on my cellular car phone and asked for Joe Casale, showroom manager. My heart went out to Joe—tiny misshapen "pinhead," flipper-like forearms.

"Joe Casale."

"Joe, this is Mark Leyner. I was in about an hour ago to test-drive the new Capri and I think I left a book on the passenger seat. Can you have someone check and see if it's there?"

"No problem, Mr. Leyner. Just hold for a couple of seconds."

"Thanks, babe."

A minute or two passed and Casale returned to the line.

"Mr. Leyner, I'm sorry but the Capri you drove is out on the road again. Where are you now?"

"I'm at the Hyatt Self-Surgery Clinic in New Brunswick."

"I'll tell you what, Mr. Leyner, why don't I drop the book off at the clinic later this evening."

"It's not out of your way?"

"It's no problem, Mr. Leyner."

"Thanks, babe."

I parked, slung my overnight bag over my shoulder, and went in to register. The clerk at the front desk keyed my name and American Express number into the computer.

"Mr. Leyner, what procedure will you be performing on yourself?"

I hesitated for a moment before responding. It seemed injudicious to divulge to this woman that a deceased rodent was impacted between my prostate gland and urethra and that the surgical procedure I intended to perform was a radical gerbilectomy.

"Appendectomy," I lied.

"Mr. Leyner, do you have a preference with regard to O.R. accommodations?"

"Well, where do the real players stay?"

"The 'real players,' sir?"

I pushed my sunglasses down the bridge of my nose and superciliously eyeballed the desk clerk over the blue mirrored lenses.

"The players . . . the Stephen Kings, the Louis L'Amours, the Jeffrey Archers, and Ken Folletts and James Clavells."

"Mr. L'Amour was in last month to perform his own cold-fusion blepharoplasty and he stayed in . . . let me check . . . ah yes, the Tivoli Suite."

"I would like the Tivoli Suite, then."

"Very good, sir."

*   *   *

It's 10:30 P.M. I'm in the Tivoli Suite and I've just self-administered a spinal block leaving my lower torso insensible to pain. I'm about to make my first incision when I hear the doorknob turn.

"¿*Quién es?*" I ask. "Who is it?"

With the exception of my instrument tray and my lower abdomen, which are illuminated by high-powered halogen lamps, the room is pitch dark. I tilt a lamp toward the door and discern a figure with a tiny head and a copy of Edmund Spenser's *The Faerie Queene* tucked under his flipper.

"Joe?" I inquire.

"It was right on the passenger seat where you left it, Mr. Leyner!"

"Thanks, babe."

Joe turns to leave.

"Joe, wait a minute. How'd you like to come work for me?"

"Work for you, Mr. Leyner?"

"Yeah. Move into headquarters, coordinate the staff, oversee the bodyguards, y'know, do a little of this, a little of that—you'd be my adjutant, my aide-de-camp. It's a great group of people, you get free medical treatment from Dr. Larry Werther—my cousin, my gastroenterologist—and basically I think you'd do a great job and I think you'd have a ball. What do you say?"

"Mr. Leyner . . . I think you have yourself an aide-de-camp," Joe says, extending a flipper.

"Welcome aboard, babe."

You enter the pink-and-yellow-splashed foyer and you're swept quickly toward the inner sanctum. Flashbulbs pop as svelte spokesmodel and media liaison Baby Lago pours the Moët. Out of the corner of your eye, you see Arleen ravaging a french-fried yam. She's wearing a short, provocative strapless dress by Emanuel Ungaro that's candy-box pink and pale green. The dress is so provocative that you want to approach Arleen and perhaps caress the nape of her neck. But you dare not. Because there I am. Even more heavily muscled than you'd expected. More frightening and yet somehow more alluring than you'd imagined. My crisp white shirt is by Georges Marciano and costs about $88. My suede jeans—Ender Murat, $550—are rolled up, exposing calves that make you realize for perhaps the first time in your life how beautiful the human calf can actually be—when it's pumped up almost beyond recognition. I'm being interviewed by a reporter from *Allure,* the new Condé Nast beauty magazine.

"I have a way of being noticed and being mysterious at once," I'm saying, "like a gazelle that is there one second and then disappears."

Joe Casale comes running in. "Mr. Leyner, Mr. Leyner—Marla's on '20/20.' You said I should let you know."

"OK, babe, thanks. Everybody quiet down! Joe, turn it up."

"Today Marla Maples, the twenty-six-year-old model-actress who first achieved notoriety as the 'other woman' in the Donald and Ivana Trump divorce, sits on death row at San Quentin as her attorneys exhaust their final appeals in an apparently futile attempt to save the blond serial killer from the gas chamber. Implicated in the deaths of Leonard Bernstein, Malcolm Forbes, Grace Kelly, Billy Martin, Muppet-creator Jim Henson, and reggae singer Peter Tosh, Maples has devoted her final weeks to a letter-writing campaign in support of a congressional bill that will require television sets manufactured after July 1997 to be equipped with a computer chip that provides caption service for the deaf.

"Marla, you're young, you're leggy, you're busty—yet in a matter of days, the State of California is going to put you in a metal room and fill it with sodium cyanide gas. Do you have any advice for other leggy, busty, young women who might be experiencing peer pressure to experiment with serial killing and who might be watching tonight?"

"That's enough, Joe. Turn the TV off, OK? Thanks, babe."
I apologize to the *Allure* reporter.

"Now . . . where were we?"

"I was asking you how you got started as a writer, and, more specifically, how you got started writing liner notes for albums."

"When I was six, I came home from school one day and I went down into the basement to look for a bicycle pump and I found the dead bodies of my parents. They were each hanging from a noose, naked. All their fingers had been cut off and arranged in a pentagram under their dangling feet and in the center of this pentagram of bloody fingers was a note and the note said: 'Dear Mark, You did this to us.'

"A year later, I took a job as a bookkeeper at an insurance agency that was located in an old two-story brick building not far from here. And on my first day of work, a few of my colleagues took me out to lunch. After a long silence, one of them finally said that there was something very important that they needed to tell me. He said that about thirty or forty years ago, our office building had been owned by a very wealthy man. And this man was a chronic philanderer. And his wife knew about his affairs. And she decided that the only way to end his infidelity and to preserve their marriage was to get pregnant again, to have a 'change-of-life baby.' So she stopped using contraceptives and, sure enough, she got pregnant. The baby was born, a boy. And he was horribly deformed. He had neurofibromatosis—Elephant Man's disease. The couple kept the child shackled in a storeroom in the husband's commercial property. He was never brought to the couple's home, but kept for his entire childhood in a dark, windowless storage room in the very building that this insurance company now occupies. The child, the monster child, did nothing to stop the husband's philandering. In fact, if anything, the tragedy of this birth, of having to go every day to the storage room and find this chained horror writhing in its own excrement, simply deepened the husband's despair and inflamed his bitter compulsion to betray his wife. All of this finally drove the wife over the edge and one night, while the husband was working in the office building, she set it on fire. The husband's charred body was found, but somehow the deformity escaped. And although he's never been seen, it's rumored that on his birthday he goes foraging for a special meal of human flesh.

"At this point, my colleagues looked at me beseechingly and confided their suspicion that the monster child returns at night to the building. 'We're begging you,' they said, 'don't stay late. If there's extra work to be done, take it home. But there's danger—we feel it, we feel that he comes back.'

"It was soon Christmas season. And one of my responsibilities was to close out the books for the year. It was a very hectic time for us and one night I was asked by the president of the company to stay late, finish some work, and then lock up. That night I worked on the books until almost two in the morning—the building, of course, completely empty except for me. I finished up, turned out the lights, armed the building's security system, locked the door, and exited. I walked through the parking lot to my car, opened the front door, and got in. There was a smell . . . a smell of rotting flowers, of putrid water from a neglected vase . . . and the stench of decaying flesh. I felt something on my neck . . . not fingers, but stumps . . . finger stumps caressing my neck. I turned around and there were the corpses of my parents seated in the back, and they were gazing at me with wide eyes and horrible grins on their faces. I was ice-cold and nauseous with terror. I opened the car door, rolled to the ground, and ran back to the building. Fumbling frantically with the keys, I finally got the door open. I took a few trembling steps into the dark hallway, when I felt something brush against my leg and then do a series of . . . are you familiar with classical ballet steps?"

The *Allure* reporter nods. "Somewhat."

"Well, it did a series of *brisés volés.* This is a flying *brisé* where you finish on one foot after the beat and the other is crossed in back . . . it's basically a *fouetté* movement with a *jeté battu*. And then it landed in the middle of the reception area in an *arabesque à la hauteur*—that's an *arabesque* where the working leg is raised at a right angle to the hip, one arm curved over the head, the other extended to the side. It was the monster child! And he had a birthday hat on his head! To my astonishment—especially after everything I'd heard—he wasn't such a malevolent creature after all. We talked for quite a while—touching on a wide range of issues—and then he said that he had a friend who was in trouble and he asked me if I could help her. I said I'd try. I followed him deep into the woods, maybe two or three miles until we stopped. And there seated against a tree, sobbing inconsolably, was Julianne Phillips.

" 'What's wrong?' I asked her.

"She said that Bruce Springsteen had just left her for Patti Scialfa.

" 'Listen, I've got a car,' I said. 'Is there somewhere I could take you?'

" 'P-P-Paula's.'

"Well, it turned out that Paula was Paula Abdul. And we became very close. And it was through Paula that I met Elton and then Axl and Queen Latifah. And that's basically how I got started writing liner notes."

"Thank you very much, Mr. Leyner, that was absolutely fascinating!" the *Allure* reporter gushes. "And good luck on your new book."

"Thanks, it was a pleasure chatting."

I'm frequently asked that question about how I got started writing liner notes and I have to admit that it's become somewhat tedious explaining it over and over again. So I feel a bit pooped and sneak off to the bedroom for a quick nap. There's an open book on my pillow. This is one of Arleen's modes of communicating with me. She'll leave a certain book, opened to a certain page and passage, on my pillow, and I'll deduce from the text what Arleen is trying to tell me. Perhaps a passage from Wordsworth's "The Prelude," indicating that she'd like to spend more time in pristine, rural environments. Or an issue of *Vogue*, hinting that a new blouse or pair of shoes might be appreciated. Or maybe a chapter from Greenberg and Johnson's *Emotionally Focused Therapy for Couples*, implying that we're not "connecting" as Arleen feels we should be. So I take the volume—a weighty anthropology textbook—from the pillow and read the indicated passage:

When the men have retired to the "sulk house" to sulk, the youngsters run exuberantly to the river. In they wade, and with playful boasts, attempt to snare recyclable refuse—everything from broken chunks of polyvinyl chloride buoys to foil packets of ketchup—from the swift current. The women, who have been watching from either the menstrual gazebos or the song stalls where they flatten manioc cakes between their hands to rhythmic doggerel, shout praise at the boys and heap derision on the ensconced brooding men, impugning their scavaging prowess and disparaging their virility. The men sulk for usually an hour, when a preset timer resounds in the sulk house and, depending on whether the men have planned a hunting raid or just want to watch television and drink, prepare themselves accordingly. If TV and drinking comprise the agenda, the men change from their dark, cowled sulking robes into gym shorts and flip-flops and undo their topknots, letting their long orange hair fall casually down their backs. They then make exaggerated exhibitions of pride about their hair, tossing their heads and narcissistically flipping their tresses about with the backs of their hands. Although these displays of extravagant, almost effeminate vanity usually culminate in gales of laughter, this is a crucial, highly ritualized transition activity that psychologically enables the men to shift from sulking to watching television and drinking—a transition that is physically accomplished by walking through an underground passageway from the sulk house to the spirit house. Once in the spirit house, the remote control for the television—a device made out of black beeswax, parana palm thatch, jaguar bone, and toucan feather tassels and featuring power, mute, volume, and channel buttons—can only be operated by the "kakarum" (powerful one). To be acknowledged as a kakarum, a man must have killed at least several persons. It is considered a feat of overwhelming courage and strength to kill a kakarum and wrest from him jurisdiction over the remote control—but this rarely happens, and in fact none of the elder informants can remember a remote control ever being taken from a kakarum. Kakarums are believed to possess supernatural power derived from the souls of the men they have killed. The prospect of acquiring this power by killing a kakarum and usurping his remote control rights is often too enticing for ambitious young men to resist. But conflicts over the remote control almost invariably end with the violent death of the young challenger, whose body is then dumped down a metal chute that delivers it into a pit located between the menstrual gazebos and the song stalls where the victim is prepared for burial by his matrilineal grandmother or mother-in-law. The kakarum then chooses a TV program and signals the commencement of drinking by announcing, "Let us drink until we vomit" and "Drink quickly so that you may be drunk soon." The beverage that's consumed—and consumed in staggering quantities—is a beer made from masticated pupunah mash and sugar cane extract. It's produced in two versions: regular and lite, which is less filling. The first man to vomit is known as "wetcówe" (vomiting one) and it is he who goes outside the spirit house and makes a loud, dramatic display of vomiting in order to signal to the women to come join the men and "utcíwaiwa" (party). The women, having been signaled by the wetcówe, change from the drab clothes they'd been wearing in the menstrual gazebos or the song stalls into short, back-strapped sequined dresses, and they dance single file toward the spirit house chanting, "utcíwaiwa wetcówe! utcíwaiwa wetcówe!"

Having read the preceding selection, I'm initially at a loss to determine what message Arleen has intended to convey. Could she be trying to say that we should go out dancing more? Or that I have a drinking problem? Or that I'm dictatorial about what we watch on television? Or that I'm moody and sulk too much? Perhaps she's suggesting that I kill someone to enhance my supernatural powers. Or maybe—just maybe—she's trying to say that I need to get away from the rarified and glamorous world of my headquarters. Maybe Arleen, in all her psychotherapeutic wisdom, is trying to tell me to return to my roots, to re-stomp the rough-and-tumble stomping grounds of my youth.

So the next day, I went back to the old neighborhood to look up Rocco Trezza.

"Hey, man, where's Trezz? You seen Trezz around?" I asked a guy who used to hang out with Rocco and me.

The guy dismissed the question with a wave of his hand.

"Trezza's been bakin' doughnuts," he said disdainfully.

I hadn't been back to the old neighborhood for some twenty years and obviously I was no longer fluent in the local patois. But I didn't want to ask what "bakin' doughnuts" meant and seem like some kind of hick, so I just shook my head and rolled my eyes and said, "Bakin' doughnuts . . . oh man." I bid the guy adieu and walked down the street, trying to figure out what he meant—"bakin' doughnuts"? Maybe it meant he was doing nothing—cooking up a big zero every day. Maybe he was doing a lot of crack—blowing smoke rings through his mind. Or maybe he was pimping—maybe "doughnuts" stood for vaginas and "bake" meant control, exploit—taking the raw dough of young girls and parlaying it into lucrative pastry. Or maybe Rocco had hit it big—maybe "doughnuts" stood for the fat round digits in a seven-figure income. Then I thought maybe it meant that he was wasting his life away masturbating . . . maybe "doughnut" stood for the round configuration of fingers and thumb around the penis and "bakin' " was a literal reference to the heat caused by the friction of hand against dick or a figurative reference to the passion of autoeroticism.

I was so lost in thought as I rounded the corner of the street that I barreled right into a guy—didn't even see him coming. As I helped him up off the ground, I suddenly recognized him and I was so stunned that I let go and he fell back on the sidewalk.

It was Rocco. Rocco Trezza. He was older. A bit heavier in the gut. His hair had thinned out. But he was unmistakably Trezz. Same inimitable style: the thigh-high jackboots, the black latex jockstrap, the Prussian spiked helmet strapped under the chin.

"Trezz, I can't believe it . . . after all these years."

Trezz hugged me. "How's it goin', man?" he asked.

"I'm good. I'm good. I got a hit book out, my wife got $35,000 because a ceiling fell on her head while she was watching the Academy Awards, and we got a dog named Carmella."

"Carmella?"

"Yeah, Carmella . . . Trezz, it's really good to see you, babe."

"Likewise. I been reading about you."

"Hey, Trezz, I want to ask you about something."

"Ask."

"Trezz, I hear you been . . ."

I hesitated for a moment, wondering whether I should pursue it or not.

"Trezz, I hear you been bakin' doughnuts."

Rocco stared at me and I could see the fury just boiling up within him.

"Bakin' doughnuts? Bakin' doughnuts? You heard I was fuckin' bakin' doughnuts?!!"

He wrestled me down and pinned me to the sidewalk. His breath hit my face in hot gusts.

"After all these years . . . after all we've been through . . . after every fuckin' thing you and me have been through—you think that I would possibly fuckin' end up bakin' doughnuts?!! Huh?!!"

I threw him off me and we both looked at each other, sitting

there on the sidewalk. I still had no idea what it meant—"bakin'
doughnuts."

"Trezz," I said, "I didn't believe it . . . OK? I knew it was a
fuckin' lie."

"It is a fuckin' lie," he said, helping me up.

I put my arm around him, and me and Trezz walked down the
street. And it was just like the old days.

I'm sitting by my pool, which is encircled by the eight-foot,
four-ton basaltic bluestone pillars from Stonehenge's inner circle
that I bought with a portion of my latest advance from Harmony
Books, when Baby Lago brings me a fax that's just come in. It's
from Stu Gallenkamp, V.P. Marketing, Columbia Records, re:
the liner notes I'd written for George Michael's "Listen Without
Prejudice, Vol. 1." It says:

> Dear Mr. L., I just got off the phone with George. He loves the liner
> notes and in fact called them the most intense and, in a certain sense,
> the most significant liner notes he'd ever read. But he agrees with me
> on the advisability of deleting the following paragraph: "The teen-
> age baby-sitters are slathering me with Ben-Gay. I'm eleven. I've
> got this erotic fascination with the girls' armpits—it's completely
> unfocused; I don't know quite what I want to 'do' to or with their
> armpits, but I'm locked into their brunette stubble. The two girls
> shut my bedroom door, lock it, and turn out the lights. They take
> the warm pink wads of bubblegum from their mouths and affix them
> to special acupressure points on my body. They remove their tam-
> pons and smear menstrual blood on my eyelids. They shave their
> armpits and rinse their razors in a basin and we drink the hairy water
> and we chant—their Marlboros glowing in the crepuscular shadows.
> Then one of them—I think it was Felice—puts my face into her
> freshly shaven armpit, which smells slightly but deliciously of
> teenybopper b.o., and she says 'count backwards from 100' and the
> next thing I remember is waking up and it's Rosh Hashanah,
> U.S.A., in the 1990s."

At breakfast the next morning, Baby Lago informed me that we were out of turtle eggs and strawberries. I felt like driving her new Porsche 911 Turbo, so I offered to fetch the groceries myself, and she tossed me the keys and her flame-resistant driving gloves. I negotiated the concrete antiterrorist road barriers in first gear, the tachometer needle climbing toward the 6800-rpm redline. I brought the car to a complete stop where the headquarters access road meets the highway. I looked at myself in the rearview mirror . . . nice. And then I stomped on the gas, tore through the gearbox, and hit 60 mph in 4.8 seconds.

Approximately four miles west of Exit 16, outside of Wenton's Mill, I began following a 1983 light-blue Chevy Impala, Tennessee plates, traveling west on Rte. 70. My initial observation was of a male caucasian driver approximately 25–30 years of age and two passengers, a female caucasian and a female Hispanic, both approximately 25–30 years of age. As I followed the vehicle, I observed its occupants engage in almost continuous sex. The male driver was being fellated by the female caucasian, who was propped on hands and knees in the middle of the front seat. She, in turn, was enjoying vigorous cunnilingus courtesy of the female Hispanic who was supine in the passenger seat, her bare feet dangling out the window. Near Fannington, at the junction of Rte. 70 and the interstate, I observed a rearrangement within the moving vehicle: the female Hispanic climbed across the front seat and took over the wheel, the male caucasian slid to the middle, and the female caucasian repositioned to the passenger seat, and the sex resumed immediately. The male caucasian lay on his side, sucking the female Hispanic driver's nipples through her T-shirt and stimulating her clitoris with his hand, his legs scissored open, presenting his genitals to the seated female caucasian, who initiated uninhibited fellatio. I observed three subsequent realignments within the moving vehicle with only momentary hiatuses in sexual activity. Approaching Exit 3, outside of Knoll, I decided to pull the vehicle over. I attached my flashing red light to the roof of my car, and the vehicle slowed, pulling onto the shoulder of the highway. I got out of my car, approached the Impala, and gestured to the driver—at the time it was the female caucasian—to roll down her window. She did. The smell of sweat, semen, and vaginal mucus was overpowering. Half-eaten chicken wings and drumsticks, Juicy Fruit gum wrappers, crushed Marlboro packs, and empty beer cans were strewn all over the car. The occupants wore no trousers or underpants. Their pubic hair was full of potato chip crumbs.

"I'm charging you all with public lewdness," I said, and I looked at my watch in order to log the correct time on my report. It was 10:45 A.M.

The occupants looked at me and began to speak. But they didn't use words. A soft crackling sound, a kind of modulated static, issued from their mouths. I looked at my watch again. Incredibly, it was almost 12:45. Somehow two hours had passed.

The female Hispanic proffered a stick of fluorescent chewing gum. I chewed it. . . .

When I came to, I was in a hospital room. Four days had passed. Dr. Larry Werther, Baby Lago, Joe Casale, Rocco Trezza, and Carmella were pacing around my bed. I had a severe headache.

"Where are the bodyguards?" I asked.

"They're out in the hall, Mr. Leyner," Joe Casale said, as he worked the remote control on a television set cantilevered from the wall opposite my bed.

"What about Arleen?"

"She's got clients till ten, then I'll pick her up and bring her over."

"Larry, what was in that chewing gum?"

"When they pumped your stomach, Baby Lago took samples and analyzed them in the lab back at headquarters. Gas chromatography, mass spectrometry, nuclear magnetic resonance—

she did the works. It was ibotenic acid. A powerful neurotoxin —destroys nerve cells in the brain. It's a good thing Joe Casale had tailed you."

I gave Joe the thumbs-up. "Thanks, babe."

Joe turned his gaze momentarily from the TV and gestured with his flipper. "No problem, Mr. Leyner."

"Joe also found this stuffed in your mouth."

Larry handed me an ivory mah-jongg tile with the words *Vote for Iron Man Wang* engraved on one side.

"Damn . . ."

"Forget about it, man, that's Hong Kong," Trezza said, taking my hand in his. "You can't worry about that shit now. You've got your books and your liner notes to write—that's your life, man. Not chasing Iron Man Wang and his posse of hot-wired sex freaks around the world. That's chump shit, man."

That's why I loved Trezz. He always knew exactly what to say to make me feel better. I playfully snapped the elastic waistband of his black latex jockstrap.

"Trezz, y'know if you ever decide to stop bakin' dough—"

Trezz's eyes flared instantly.

". . . if you ever decide to stop doing whatever it is that you're doing, I'd love to have you come work for us over at headquarters. And that's a serious offer."

Trezz was about to respond when Joe Casale interrupted from across the room.

"Hey, Mr. Leyner!" he said, gesturing at the TV with the remote control. "Look at this—"

The Brazilian actress Sonia Braga, Elle MacPherson, two Victoria's Secret models, and Claudia Schiffer, the German model featured in Guess? jeans ads, were sitting around talking about what kind of man turns them on the most.

"I like a guy about five-seven," said MacPherson.

"Yeah," said Braga in husky, heavily accented English, "five-seven and about a hundred and thirty pounds."

One of the Victoria's Secret models, a voluptuous redhead in burnished gold satin and black lace demi-cup bra and bikini, was staring into space as she conjured her ultimate turn-on. "Light brown hair . . . and balding."

"Oooooh yeah . . . balding!" enthused the other Victoria's Secret model breathily. She sported a black velvet bustier and leather miniskirt.

"My *Liebchen* must have some broken blood vessels on his nose and he must be bowlegged," said the pouting Guess? jeans model, squirming a bit in her chair as she spoke.

MacPherson was distractedly tracing abstract figures in the rug when she looked up and announced: "To really turn me on so that I just melt, a man must have an irritable colon and epaulet-like patches of hair on his shoulders."

"A muscular upper body, skinny legs, and really small feet—about a size seven," Braga asserted.

The German cover girl vigorously nodded her assent. "And hazel eyes and a mole in the right eyebrow," she added.

The others swooned in unison. "Oh yes, a mole in the right eyebrow!"

The auburn-maned Victoria's Secret model had shut her eyes. Her hands were crossed over her breasts as she swayed from side to side. "I can even picture what he's wearing," she whispered. "He's got a leather blazer on over an Oakland A's T-shirt, black jeans . . ."

". . . and snakeskin boots!" MacPherson growled.

"Yes! Yes! Yes!" squealed everyone.

CHAPTER THREE

Todd was fidgeting nervously with one of the strings of his green paper smock when Dr. William Carlos Williams entered the examination room.

"Hi, Todd," Dr. Williams said.

"Hi, Dr. Williams."

"How are your folks, Todd?"

"Well, my dad was just made chairman of the Senate Armed Services Committee—but I guess you saw that on TV—and Mom is curating an exhibit of Viking jewelry at the Smithsonian."

"And how are you doing—have you finished graduate school?"

"Yeah, I finished grad school last June."

"Are you working?"

"No . . . I'm not really sure what I want to do yet, so I've just been hanging around, really . . . doing a lot of reading . . . and stuff."

"What's your degree in, Todd?"

"I've got two. I've got a master's degree in Norse mythology and a master's in chemical weapons. The trouble is that I'm not really interested in specializing in one or the other, so I'd like to try to find some kind of job that combines both fields . . . but I'm not really sure what that is . . . so I've just been kind of a couch potato lately . . . mostly reading, watching TV . . ."

"And to what do I owe the pleasure of your visit today? What seems to be bothering you?"

"Well, a couple of weeks ago I started noticing that my hands were numb every morning. And soon they began to really hurt—my hands and my wrists. It was really awful pain. It felt like someone was squeezing and twisting my nerves with a pliers."

Dr. Williams took Todd's hands in his. Todd winced.

"The pain's really that bad, huh, Todd?" Dr. Williams asked gently.

"It's really terrible."

"Does it hurt when I do this?"

"No, not so much."

"How about this?"

"A little, but not so bad."

"How about this?"

Todd howled with pain, tears welling in his eyes.

"OK, son, why don't you get dressed and come into my office. I'd like to talk to you."

Dr. Williams washed his hands in the sink and exited, closing the door behind him. Todd put his clothes on and poked his head out the door.

"Nurse, should I go into the doctor's office now or wait until he comes back?"

"No, Todd," said the pretty nurse, "you can go right in now."

Dr. Williams was seated behind a burnished mahogany desk, writing something with a Mont Blanc pen. On the wall, there was a large painting by LeRoy Neiman of a macrophage ingesting salmonella bacteria.

"Todd, have a seat," he said, signing the document with a flourish and placing it on a stack of other documents.

"Todd, how do you occupy your time? What sorts of things do you do?"

"Well, I don't do too much of anything, really . . . mainly reading and watching TV and stuff."

"Do you do anything athletic, participate in any kind of sports?"

"Not really."

"Is there anything you do with your hands, anything that you do over and over again that you think might be contributing to this pain?"

"Not really."

"Todd, I want you to think very carefully. Is there anything—I don't care how trivial or silly you might think it is—that you do with your hands or wrists repeatedly every day?"

"Well . . . there is . . . I'm kind of ashamed . . . I . . ."

Todd made a loose fist and gestured up and down.

"Masturbation, Todd?"

"Yes, Dr. Williams."

"That's what I thought, Todd. Todd, there's absolutely nothing wrong with masturbation in and of itself. It's perfectly normal behavior. About how often do you masturbate?"

"A lot."

"What's a lot?"

"Well, it's hard to count—maybe thirty or forty times a day. I do it all day. I ejaculate and then I just keep stroking until I get an erection and then I stroke until I ejaculate and then I start all over again."

"All day without stopping?"

"Well, I break for meals, but if it's a food I can eat with one hand . . ."

"Todd, do you have a girlfriend?"

"No, Dr. Williams. It's really been tough finding someone I can really talk to. I'll meet a girl who's really into chemical weapons but she won't know anything about Norse mythology and then I'll meet a girl who's really up on the mythology—she'll know everything about Odin and the Valkyries and Rodmar and Thor and Valhalla—but then she'll think that mustard gas is something you get from eating too many hot dogs."

Dr. Williams smiled.

"Todd, have you ever heard of something called carpal tunnel syndrome?"

"No, Dr. Williams."

"Carpal tunnel syndrome is a repetitive motion injury. It's also called a cumulative trauma disorder. I'll be giving you some literature about this so you don't have to remember all the jargon. In carpal tunnel syndrome, a fast repetitive motion, over time, damages the nerves and tendons in the hands and wrists. Come over here and let me show you on this model. The tendons over here, which pass through this narrow channel of wrist bones—the carpal tunnel—swell and press on this nerve here, which is called the median nerve. That's what's causing your pain and numbness. This disorder is found most frequently in people who work in meat-packing plants and poultry slaughterhouses—employees in chicken-processing plants, for instance, must make difficult cuts 60 or even 90 times a minute. And more and more, we're finding carpal tunnel syndrome in word processors—people who are hitting keys tens of thousands of times an hour. Given the frequency and duration of your masturbation, you're making the same forceful strokes 180 times a minute. That's 10,800 forceful strokes an hour . . ."

He tapped the multiplication out on his calculator.

". . . and that's 86,400 forceful strokes a day, given an eight-hour day of masturbating, which may be conservative in your case, Todd."

"Is there anything they can do about it? I mean, pills or an operation?"

"I'm going to schedule an appointment for you with my friend Herb Horowitz. He's one of the best musculoskeletal men in the business. And if, having examined you, he agrees, I'd like to schedule you for surgery."

"Surgery?" Todd said, looking frightened.

"With surgery we can take some of that pressure off the nerve—remember the median nerve I showed you?—and that can relieve the numbness and pain that you're experiencing. But that's not going to solve the problem entirely. We've got to eliminate or at least drastically cut down the forceful repetitive strokes you're making."

Todd looked glum.

"I don't think that's going to be easy, Dr. Williams."

"Look, Todd—first of all, I'd like to get you into a group. Y'know, you're not the only one going through this."

Dr. Williams handed Todd a glossy brochure entitled "The Auto-Erotic Repetitive Motion Disorder Association of America." It had a photo of a bunch of nerdy guys sitting around with various sorts of bandages and slings and splints on their hands, wrists, and arms.

"Dr. Williams, what if the therapy doesn't work and I can't stop? What then? What's the worst-case scenario?"

"We'll have to have you fixed."

"Fixed?" Todd said, his voice cracking.

"Relax, Todd. You said it yourself—it's a worst-case scenario.

Now let's take this one step at a time. I want you to see Herb Horowitz next week and let's see what our next move is, OK?"

"OK, Dr. Williams. Thanks."

Todd walked out of Dr. Williams's office with the brochure under his arm.

William Carlos Williams, respected physician *and* distinguished poet, turned to the computer keyboard at the side of his desk and began to type, trying to compose a few lines—perhaps even a stanza—before his next patient arrived.

"That was great, Mr. Leyner! Really great!" Joe Casale said, tucking a flipper under his pillow and nestling into a fetal curl. "What book is that from?"

"That's from a book called *Lives of the Poets,*" I said, showing Joe the cover before I turned off the lamp on his night table.

"Mr. Leyner, do you think I could borrow it sometime?"

"I'll tell you what, babe—tomorrow I have to be at a store downtown to sign some books. I'll pick you up a copy of your own."

(The book I was scheduled to sign—which had just been published by Rizzoli—was a $75 oversized volume of nude photographs of myself taken by a spy satellite in geostationary orbit over New Jersey. Annie Leibowitz, famed *Rolling Stone* photojournalist, upon learning that the satellite was capable of providing high-resolution images down to the brand name on a golf ball, contacted the Department of Defense and suggested that they collaborate with her on a book of photographs of me lolling about the headquarter's rooftop patio, au naturel, basted with oil, and flexing.)

Joe started getting out of bed. "Mr. Leyner, let me give you some money."

"Forget about it, babe. It's on me. It'll be a token of appreciation for the job you're doing here at headquarters. Don't think I haven't noticed. You're up every morning at five A.M. walking Carmella, helping Trezz train the bodyguards, making sure Baby

Lago has everything she needs for the commissary. You're taking care of business . . . and I'm proud of you."

"Thanks, Mr. Leyner."

"Bon soir, babe."

Arleen was in bed listening to a Fordham lacrosse game on her Walkman. There were a couple of fan letters on my pillow. I receive a tremendous amount of fan mail every day. It's one of Baby Lago's responsibilities to screen the letters, respond to those that are simply requests for nude photos and swatches of un-washed T-shirts and Jockey briefs, turn any threats over to Joe or Trezz and the security team, and pass along to me those that require a personal response. I slid into bed and began perusing my mail. A fan from Philadelphia, Pennsylvania, wrote:

> I am a psychic Italian-American woman who recently had cosmetic breast-and-buttock-augmentation surgery. I became psychic as a teenager after suffering from accidental carbon monoxide poisoning when I was a guest on "American Bandstand." For a period of time I was the Vatican. I am a zealot by nature and tend to become fanatically obsessive about my activities. These activities have in-cluded LSD research and Hummel collecting. During the period in which I was doing a lot of acid, I supported myself by ghost-writing poetry for some of the most acclaimed poets in the country including Randall Jarrell and Robert Lowell. When it was discovered that John Kennedy was obsessed with my body during the Cuban Missile Crisis, the CIA had my breasts and buttocks surgically reduced. Today I live on a quiet tree-lined suburban street. My husband is a kind man and a good provider, but I find him terribly insipid. His way of trying to be more romantic is to be more obsequious and I find that a real turnoff. While he's away at work during the day, I've begun seeing a large black policeman with a shaved head. My ques-tion is this: The policeman (whom I'll call "Nightstick" to protect his family) knows all about a sexual fantasy that a number of years ago I'd sent to Nancy Friday for her book *My Secret Garden*. Friday had assured all contributors that their submissions would be kept

absolutely confidential. How did "Nightstick" find out about this
fantasy and what is my legal recourse vis-à-vis Nancy Friday and her
publishing company?

Yours truly, Francine Masiello

I was scheduled to meet the manager of the Global Entertainment—Book, Record, & Video Annex at 11 A.M. the next morning. As I entered the store, I was pleased to see an elaborate window display of the book of photographs, which Rizzoli had entitled *The Celestial Voyeur: Heavenly Views of an Earthly Body*. The manager, a knowledgeable-looking, earnest young man in sweater and tie, was assisting a customer.

"Can I help you?" he asked.

"Yes," she said. "There's a new album out, I'm not sure what the name of it is . . . but it's the sound of two men lifting tremendous weights. I wish I could remember the name of it . . . oh shit, I was just talking about it to someone and now I can't think of it. Goddamn it!"

"Well, there are two new albums out—one is the sound of the weights themselves—the clanking of the iron plates on the barbells and the thud of dumbbells being dropped. And the other is the sounds, the vocalizations, of the men themselves."

"Is the first one just the sounds of free weights—you said barbells and dumbbells—that made it sound like only free weights? Or does it have sounds from a Universal or Nautilus? Like I wonder if it's got the sound of the metal pin going into the right weight slot on the rack?"

"I think it's free weights, Universal, Nautilus, stationary bike, and Stairmaster all mixed together—sampled. But just the sounds of the equipment, not people."

"No, I think it's the other one—the men. I think it's called something like *Smell My Thick Leather Belt After I Power-Lift* . . . or maybe *Hymns to a Hernia, Huge Weights and Sweaty Straining Men* . . . or something like *Colossal Men Suckle Methyltestosterone*

49

from the Hairy Nipples of the Men Who Spot for Them or something like that."

"Let me see here . . . OK, we have something called *Getting Huge—The Incredible Sounds of Hairy Men in Thick Leather Belts Lifting Tremendous Weights: A Sonic Mosaic of Pain, Nipples, Armpit Hair, Sweat, and Protein Powder.*"

"Is it a Nonesuch album?"

"Yes. Nonesuch."

"That's it! That I remember, Nonesuch is the label. You have the CD, right?"

"We sure do."

"Good, because I think they said on the radio that the CD has two cuts that the cassette doesn't have."

"That's right, the CD includes one cut with the sounds of the two men doing rear-delt cable laterals and another cut with them doing crossover flys with extremely heavy weights."

"Is that the one where you hear one guy saying, 'C'mon, let's get big, let's get big,' and the other starts his reps and you hear him moan and then the other guy starts screaming at him, 'Move the weight! You're a fuckin' strong man, you're an animal! Burn it, burn it!' and then the other guy growls as he completes his set and then at the end you hear them give each other high-fives?"

"Yeah."

"Well, I definitely think that's the one I heard on Public Radio. Do you carry video equipment and computer equipment?"

"Yes, we do."

"OK, there's something, I'm not exactly sure what it is—some kind of interactive computerized laser video player or interactive digital video software or something—but it enables you to take any movie and insert Arnold Schwarzenegger as the actor in the lead role . . ."

"Yes, we have what you're talking about, but you're a little confused about it. We have the equipment here: the computer, the digital video image synthesizing unit, the software—all that—we have that in the store. You tell us what you want—which films you want Schwarzenegger inserted into and we do it right here for you."

"So you do it—I don't need to buy the equipment?"

"Oh no no no, we do it right here. As a matter of fact, you can even fax your order in and we'll deliver the Schwarzeneggerized videos to your home."

"Oh cool! Can I order some now?"

"Sure."

"OK. I'd like *My Fair Lady* with Arnold Schwarzenegger as Professor Henry Higgins, *Amadeus* with Arnold Schwarzenegger as Salieri instead of F. Murray Abraham, *The Diary of Anne Frank* with Arnold Schwarzenegger as Anne Frank, *West Side Story* with Arnold Schwarzenegger as Tony, *It's a Wonderful Life* with Arnold Schwarzenegger instead of Jimmy Stewart, *Gandhi* with Arnold Schwarzenegger instead of Ben Kingsley, *Bird* with Arnold Schwarzenegger as Charlie Parker instead of Forest Whitaker . . . can you do documentaries?"

"Sure."

"There's a documentary called *Imagine* about John Lennon. Could you fix it so that it's Arnold Schwarzenegger instead of Lennon?"

"No problem."

"So it'll be Schwarzenegger playing with the Beatles on Ed Sullivan and Schwarzenegger doing those peace things in bed with Yoko Ono and everything?"

"Yes, ma'am. Our equipment is state of the art."

"OK, and one last one . . . how about *Rain Man?*"

"Would you like Arnold Schwarzenegger as the autistic brother or the Tom Cruise character?"

"Could you do it so he's both, sort of like Patty Duke did as Patty/Cathy in 'The Patty Duke Show'?"

"We can, yes . . . that may be a little more expensive, though."

51

"Well, I'll take it. And I think that's it, and thank you very much for all your help."

"It's been my pleasure," said the earnest young man.

Occasionally, I'll conduct a writing workshop. I'm accompanied by my phalanx of bionic elderly bodyguards, some of whom are heavily armed and stationed at predetermined strategic positions within the room and building, and some of whom work undercover, posing as workshop participants. I'm also armed. Since I don't like to carry a firearm when I conduct a writing workshop—I've found that it tends to inhibit people who haven't yet developed a confident style of their own—I'll come with an icepick in my sock. I openly brandish a cargo hook, but I figure that in the event that somehow someone is able to wrest the cargo hook from me, I'll have recourse to the hidden icepick.

I usually start the workshop by showing slides in response to questions. Thanks to the media attention that's been focused on my car collection, someone inevitably asks about my most recent automotive acquisition. So, for instance, at the last workshop I taught, I showed slides of my newest car, which is made by Visigoth Motor Works (VMW), a survivalist automobile manufacturer located in northern Idaho. I've got their sports coupe, the Piranha 793 (commemorating the year that Viking raiders sacked the English monastery of Lindisfarne). It features state-of-the-art technology that not only protects its passengers in the event of a collision, but ensures the death of the passengers in the other car. The Piranha 793 is the perfect automotive statement for the "I'm OK, You're Lunch" generation. It incorporates computerized infrared homing systems that guide the vehicle toward the heat generated by the engine of an oncoming car, ensuring head-on collisions with "optimized lethality."

Climaxing my slide presentation, I showed a photograph that I thought perfectly captured the glamour and éclat of Visigoth

Motor Works: it's me arriving at the People's Choice Awards in my Piranha 793 convertible, almost anonymous in my Kevlar driving mask, were it not for the bare-midriff football jersey revealing my inimitably ripped abdominals.

After the Q and A, I'll pose a question to the workshop participants: Do any of you think you could ever be as good a writer as I am—or perhaps even a better writer—and would you explain why you feel the way you do. Yes—over there, the fellow in the green sweater.

"Well, I think it's possible—although it would take just a tremendous, tremendous amount of work to reach your level of virtuosity—I think it's possible that I could someday be as good a writer as you are, although a very different kind of writer. I've lived all over the world and I've had a very interesting life, full of passion and joy and a great deal of sadness and pain, and I think that if I could ever develop a style to accommodate all the material that I've stored in my head and in my heart, I could be a damn interesting novelist."

"OK . . . anyone else? The lady in the back with the boots and the vest."

"Well, yes, Mr. Leyner, although I have a great deal of respect and admiration for your accomplishments, I certainly think that my work has as much literary validity as yours does. I've studied with some very fine writers at various programs around the country and I've worked assiduously at my craft for a good number of years now and etc. etc. etc."

A couple of other people will affirm themselves and proclaim their ambitions, and then I'll ask if there's anyone else and, if not, we'll proceed with some writing exercises.

At the conclusion of the workshop, my bodyguards, who've been working undercover, will take into custody each of those participants who has stated that he or she could be as good a writer as I am. Quietly, so as not to alarm those who have remained to get my autograph, the detained participants are handcuffed, loaded into the security van, and taken to headquarters. The standard procedure begins with the placing of a bag over a detainee's head; interrogation and reeducation can last from several hours to a few weeks. Sleep deprivation, exposure to cold, mock executions, and various psychological techniques are used to persuade the detainees never to write again. When the staff is certain that a detainee's reeducation is complete, the detainee is branded on the buttocks with my insignia as a reminder of his matriculation at headquarters and then released. It's the antithesis of a writer's colony, an anti-Yaddo.

Bookstore shelf-space is limited, as are the column inches available in today's book reviews, and we at headquarters are adamant in our belief that all competition—active or potential— must be neutralized.

My insignia is a guy surfing on an enormous wave of lava—it's an avalanche of this lurid molten spume with this glowering chiseled commando in baggy polka-dotted trunks on an iridescent board careering across the precipice of this incredible fuming tsunami of lava—and there's an erupting volcano in the distance in the upper right-hand corner. It's excellent.

I have it tattooed on my heart. And I don't mean on the skin of my chest over my heart. I mean tattooed on the organ itself. It's illegal in the States—I had to go to Mexico. It's called visceral tattooing. They have to open you up. They use an ink that contains a radioactive isotope so that the tattoo shows up on X-rays and CAT scans.

Do you want to get sick to your stomach—I'll describe the fetid, vermin-infested office of the "physician" who did my first visceral tattoo: Dr. José Fleischman. I went to sit down on what I thought was a couch in his waiting room . . . it wasn't a couch. It was thousands—tens of thousands—of cockroaches that had gathered in a mass that was the shape of a couch. The same thing happened with what I thought was a magazine. I reached for what I thought was the latest issue of *Sports Illustrated* and it moved. It wasn't a magazine at all, but a rectangular swarm of centipedes with a cluster of silverfish lying near the upper edge, and I guess from a distance, and in the dim light, the silverfish against the dark background of centipedes looked as if they formed the words *Sports Illustrated.* There was no receptionist and there were no other clients.

Finally, Fleischman emerged from the back room. The lenses of his eyeglasses were the thickest I'd ever seen. They actually bulged several inches out from the frames. It was as if he were wearing two of those snow-filled glass paperweights on his face. His clothes were soaked through with sweat. I explained that I wanted a surfer on a wave of molten lava tattooed on my heart and I handed him a color Xerox of my insignia. He lit a cigarette and studied the rendering from various angles, holding his head askew and squinting through the smoke.

"My friend," he said, speaking for the first time, "what chamber?"

"Chamber?" I asked.

He pointed with his cigarette to a yellowing diagram on the wall.

"The two atria are thin-walled. The ventricles are thick-walled. I recommend the ventricles. Either one—it's your call, *amigo.*"

I scrutinized the diagram for a few seconds.

"The left ventricle," I announced.

"Bueno," said Fleischman. "Today, we gonna put you out, open you up, and I'm gonna just do the outlines, then I sew you up. Then in two weeks, we open again, we fill in the colors, and sew up, all finished."

I was still looking over the diagram.

"Say, Fleischman, while you got me on the table, could you do 'Mom' on my pulmonary artery?"

"What kind of calligraphy you like? You like somethin' like this?"

He showed me an X-ray of someone's thyroid gland with the word *Mother* done in what he called "Florentine style"—a very serpentine, filigreed style of lettering.

"That's very nice." I nodded.

Those were my first visceral tattoos. I've had many since. A tip to the guys out there—visceral tattoos really turn on female medical technicians and nurses. I've had numerous hot relationships start because a med-tech or a nurse saw one of my X-rays and went nuts over all the tattoos. They know that any wimp can go out and get "Winona Forever" stenciled on his arm—but it takes real balls to have yourself put under general anesthesia, sliced open, have a vital organ etched with radioactive isotope ink, and then get sewn up again every time you want to commemorate that special lady.

Next, I want to have the words *Desert Storm—Thunder and Lightning* tattooed on my left frontal cortex. But I don't know where I'm going to go for that one. Brain tattooing is illegal even in Mexico. Someone told me maybe Malaysia.

Rocco left today. Baby Lago and I found a mercenary magazine left open on his bed with a page torn out. I was surprised, but not surprised, if you know what I mean. Lately, he'd seemed uncharacteristically subdued. He'd been talking a lot about his father. That in itself struck me as peculiar. Trezz wasn't typically given to retrospection or wistfulness. But every so often I'd find him smoking a cigar by one of the bay windows overlooking the carp ponds and I'd say, "Trezz, what's up, man?" and he'd gaze into the distance for a minute or two and then he'd take the cigar out of his mouth and stare at the soggy masticated stub and he'd say in a hoarse whisper: "I was thinkin' about my old man."

Rocco's father had been a medical cheese sculptor—he sculpted cheese centerpieces for medical conventions. It was a profession that required not only fine craftsmanship and an encyclopedic knowledge of cheeses, but a comprehensive understanding of human anatomy. One needed to know which cheeses by dint of their hues and textures would allow the sculptor to render an organ with maximum fidelity. Havarti with dill, for instance, is particularly suitable for sculpting uterine lining. Mozzarella has just the right slickness and convoluted folds for the brain. A long and difficult apprenticeship is necessary. Rocco's father studied with a master medical cheese sculptor for over ten years before he was allowed to solo, debuting with a cheddar prostate gland for the American Society of Urologists 1937 convention in Lake Tahoe. Tragically, at the height of his career, there was a terrible accident. Rocco's father and mother had won a sweepstakes contest and had gone to London, England. One night they went to a pub. And the poor man, not knowing the local customs, walked where he shouldn't have and took a dart in the right temple. He survived, but his virtuosity with a cheese knife was irrevocably lost. A proud man, he stubbornly refused to capitulate, attempting to recover some vestige of dexterity through a daily regimen of physical therapy, until age and infirmity made even that impossible. Rocco was at his bedside when he died. He had something in his fist and before the body was removed from the hospital room, Rocco gently pried open his fingers to see what he'd been gripping with such poignant tenacity: it was a torn anterior cruciate ligament made out of Muenster and Swiss that he'd been laboring to complete for the Canadian Association of Sports Physicians' 25th Annual Meeting in Ottawa. Trezz kept his father's final sculpture with him always, and when he came to work at headquarters he stored it in a special place in the commissary freezer.

We checked the freezer this afternoon; the Muenster and Swiss ligament was gone, along with Rocco.

In the middle of the night, the phone rings.

Arleen answers.

I roll over and go back to sleep.

I'm in the middle of a dream. I'm leaning out the window of my car, kissing a tollbooth attendant. She's savoring my mouth with her tongue and gently biting my lips and sighing and her kissing is so sweet and languorous that it's breaking my heart. Traffic is at a complete standstill for over fifteen miles.

Arleen nudges me awake.

"It's for you, babe," she says.

"Who is it?" I ask.

Arleen inquires.

"It's a woman named Desiree Buttcake."

"I don't know anyone named Desiree Buttcake. If it's a fan calling about the solid-gold belt buckle custom-minted with the lava-surfer insignia and the words *Team Leyner,* tell her to call the 800 number."

"C'mon, Mark, she say she knows you. Take the phone—I want to go back to sleep."

I take the phone.

"Hello, this is Mark Leyner."

"Hi, Mark, this is Desiree Buttcake."

"Desiree, I'm sorry, but I don't really know who you are."

She laughs.

"Mark, of course you don't know me . . . well, I mean you don't know me as Desiree Buttcake . . . you know me as Francine Masiello. I wrote you a letter a couple of weeks ago. I'm the psychic who recently had cosmetic breast-and-buttock-augmentation surgery . . . remember?"

"Oh yeah . . . you're the Hummel collector who got carbon monoxide poisoning on 'American Bandstand.' "

"That's right, that's me."

"Well, what's up, Francine . . . I mean, Desiree."

"I want to work for you, Mark. And I want to start tonight. There are important things I can do for you and your organization, but they need to be discussed immediately."

"Well, listen, Desiree, applicants for employment at headquarters usually have to undergo an extremely rigorous interview process and security check."

"Interview me tonight. It's critical that I start working for you as soon as possible, believe me."

"OK, where are you?"

"Every Thursday night a cell of right-wing intellectuals, novelists, playwrights, poets, painters, architects, and psychics meet in the sauna of a different Jack LaLanne Health Spa. The location of the sauna is kept secret from members of the cabal until 9:40 P.M. on Thursday night at which time it's announced in an encrypted fax. Let's see here . . . OK, tonight we're meeting in the sauna at the Jack LaLanne Health Spa in the Linwood Mall, Fort Lee, New Jersey."

"I'll be there," I say.

When I arrive at the Jack LaLanne Health Spa, there is no sign that a clandestine meeting of ultra-right-wing intellectuals and psychics is taking place in its sauna. Yelping aerobics classes, the echo of racquetballs, sweaty florid-faced hausfraus in garish leotards slumped at juice machines, men with hairy jiggling breasts and gelatinous rolls of stretch-marked belly fat grimly tramping on treadmills and Stairmasters—nothing out of the ordinary. I undress in the locker room, walk down a short hallway, come to a door marked SAUNA and open it. Through the thick steam, the first face I recognize is that of Dr. Claude Lorphelin, a gynecologist, surrealist poet, and neo-fascist pamphleteer who lives in the posh 16th Arrondissement of the Paris, France, simulation at Epcot Center.

"*Bonjour,* Dr. Lorphelin," I say, extending my hand into the fog.

A latex surgical glove emerges, gripping my hand.

"*Bonjour,* Monsieur Leyner. We are very happy to see you. Your article was magnificent."

"*Merci,*" I say, acknowledging the concordant murmurs of approbation with a crisp bow of the head.

Lorphelin was referring to an article I'd written deploring the fecklessness, physical cowardice, and political disloyalty of the current literary community. Published on the Op-Ed page of the *New York Times,* the article exhorted artists to stop their incessant whining; to stop crawling on their knees with their hands out, begging for grant money and fellowships; to stop exalting self-marginalization; to emerge from their academic sanctuaries where they huddle like shivering, squinting, runty, sexless, nihilistic mice—to emerge into the intoxicating, palpitating, nutrient-rich sunlight of the marketplace, to intermix with the great people of a great nation, and to be emboldened by the truculent spirit of the populace.

"Mark, over here," a woman's voice emerges from the corner.

"Desiree, is that you, babe?"

"It's me. Listen, why don't we go somewhere where we can conduct our interview more privately."

"OK. There's a diner across the street. I'll meet you there in ten minutes."

I turn to say good-bye to Lorphelin.

"*Au revoir,* babe. If I'm ever in Orlando . . ."

Lorphelin stands and salutes me.

"Until Victory!" he says.

* * *

"**M**iss, I'll just have a cup of black coffee. Desiree, do you want anything?"

"I'll have a scoop of vanilla ice cream with cough suppressant whip and a cup of PMS tea."

The waitress left and Desiree rummaged in her gym bag, extracting a resumé, which she handed me across the table.

"Hmmmmmm, very impressive," I said, perusing her vita. "Captain of the Ossining High School track team, played 'ancient instruments' in the high school orchestra, Student Council President, President of Thespians and Yearbook, National Merit Scholar, combined SAT scores of 1590, attended Princeton University, spent junior year in Papua New Guinea, graduated summa cum laude, attended Yale Law, editor of Law Review, hired right out of law school by Swazy, Cummings and Bass, made full partner in six months, elected president of the American Bar Association at the age of twenty-six, appointed Attorney General of the United States by President Hallux Valgus—a post you left after a year to become a Supreme Court Justice—a position which you in turn resigned after eight months to race Formula One cars in international competition including the Monaco Grand Prix, which you won for three consecutive years . . . very, very impressive, Desiree."

"Thank you, Mark."

"There are a couple of questions I'd like to ask you. It says here that you played 'ancient instruments' in the high school orchestra . . . what exactly are ancient instruments?"

(Desiree seemed unflustered by the question and I made note of her poise in the margin of her resumé.)

"When an orchestra performs a piece of music that was written in a certain era, it's best to perform that piece using coeval, autochthonous instruments, as opposed to modern instruments— that is to say, instruments of that era and region, the instruments for which the music was presumably written. Most high school orchestras can't afford ancient instruments, but I was quite fortunate in that Ossining High was a particularly well-endowed school, and to give you an example: in my senior year we performed an orchestral piece written in 3000 B.C. by a Mesopotamian composer; I played an instrument which consists of the inflated bladder of an emu, which is either scraped with a bone plectrum or bowed with stiffened flax fibers. It produces an extraordinary plaintive tone quite unlike anything else I've ever heard."

(I found Desiree's response to be forthright and thoughtful, and again jotted down my evaluation.)

"Desiree, you stepped down as Attorney General after only a year and then stepped down as a Supreme Court Justice after only eight months. Do you think that this exhibits an immature restlessness and inability to honor long-term commitments or do you think that it exhibits a wonderful kind of boundless, nomadic intelligence and creativity that can't and shouldn't be constrained by a single vocation?"

"The latter."

(Very direct, succinct, confident.)

"Desiree, what sort of position are you looking for with us?"

"Something in security. As you can see, I've been in some dangerous situations and I think that my experience would be a great asset to you and your staff. As I alluded to on the phone, I definitely think you need to beef up your security, and now. There are rumors out there about missing fiction workshop participants . . . things could get rough."

(There was now positively no doubt in my mind that Desiree would be an invaluable addition to the staff at headquarters, and I made a note of my decision.)

"Could you start tomorrow?"

"Absolutely!" she said, grinning.

"Good. We'll see you at nine A.M. Report to Baby Lago and she'll see that you get your W-2 forms and security pass and health insurance information and belt buckle. OK? Desiree, I've got to get going now, Arleen's going to be worried about me. Welcome to Team Leyner."

I stood up, kissed her on the cheek, and threw some money on the table.

"Mark, there's one more thing I want to talk to you about. Do you do drugs? There's something I think you might be interested in."

I sat back down.

"Desiree, as you know, Mark Leyner is about total fitness and power—muscle mass, density, ripped definition, triceps, biceps, pecs, lats, glutes, intensity, stamina, endurance, mental focus . . . on the other hand, I do have a responsibility to my fans to forge ahead where most men fear to tread. I mean, we can't leave the exploration of inner space to New Age Milquetoasts like Terence McKenna. What kind of drug and how much?"

"Well, it's not really a 'drug' per se, although it'll get you off, believe me. And I don't exactly have it to sell you, but I know you'll be interested and I know how you can get it. It's Lincoln's morning breath."

"What's 'morning breath'?"

"Y'know, it's the worst breath of the day—morning breath."

"Lincoln's morning breath? Abraham Lincoln's morning breath?"

"There's a vial of Lincoln's morning breath in the National Museum of Health and Medicine in Washington, D.C. The museum used to be the Medical Museum of the Armed Forces Institute of Pathology and it's located on the grounds of the Walter Reed Army Medical Center. They've got thousands of specimens, including tissue samples from presidents and military leaders. But when I heard about this, a sealed ampule of Lincoln's morning breath—I mean a snort or two and who knows—I knew you'd be interested, Mark."

"Desiree, I think this is going to be a very profitable association for both of us. See you in the A.M., babe."

I stood up again, turned to leave, and then remembered something that had been on my mind.

"Desiree, in your letter you said something about being the Vatican. Did you mean the building?"

"Yeah, the building," she said.

Joe Casale made the arrangements. We've got the first-class section of Continental Flight 213 to National Airport in Washington, D.C., all to ourselves. Arleen's wearing a chartreuse skating skirt with an ornate jeweled bodice and boots with jeweled cuffs. I'm wearing Air Jordans, camouflage pants, no shirt, an onyx quarter-pound burger embedded with chunks of diamond on a gold rope around my neck, and a black baseball cap with the words *Golden Nugget* in gold stitching. When we reach cruising altitude, our stewardess rolls out a five-foot hero with mortadella, cappicola, prosciutto, sharp provolone, and sweet peppers, two bottles of Johnnie Walker Black, and a bucket of ice. We each take a bottle and start on either end of the sandwich. Arleen—by day, mender of shattered psyches; by night, voluptuous temptress and pleasure addict—is a woman of voracious appetites. By the time we make our final approach to D.C., she's polished off two feet of hero and a fifth of scotch.

As we touch down and taxi toward our gate, I nudge Arleen and flash two White House press passes.

"You said you always wanted to go to a presidential news conference, right, babe?"

"Oh, Mark!! When? When?!"

"Tomorrow morning, 1600 Pennsylvania Avenue."

Arleen is euphoric. Ever since that spring afternoon when she shot me out of a tree with a tranquilizer dart, there've been two things she's always talked about wanting to do: see harness racing at the Meadowlands and attend a presidential news conference. I've now made good on both of my nuptial promises. And she's loving it.

Q: Mr. President, I have a chunk of pork in my mouth—

A: I'm sorry, you say you have a pork chunk in your mouth?

Q: Yes. I have a chunk of pork in my mouth and I'm not planning on chewing it or swallowing it. Do you have any idea if it's possible for my saliva to dissolve the chunk and, if it is possible, can you say how long it will take for my saliva to dissolve the piece of pork? And I have a follow-up question.

A: As I've stated previously, the enzyme in saliva, amylase, functions primarily to break down carbohydrates. It's the gastric juice in the stomach that works on proteins . . . it's the pepsin, which is the stomach's main digestive enzyme, and the hydrochloric acid in the gastric juice that will really break down the pork chunk. But it may very well be that the saliva in your mouth over a long period of time could possibly erode the chunk away . . . We'll have to get back to you with some more information on that.

Q: My follow-up question is this: There's been a tremendous amount of controversy recently about the size of the First Lady. At a briefing last week, your press secretary—in response to a question about how you first met her—said that you were at an after-hours club, sitting next to a man who still had anti-shoplifting magnetic tags attached to his sports jacket and safari shorts. Now the FBI is baffled as to how this man managed to leave the Harvé Benard outlet in Takoma Park with anti-shoplifting magnetic tags affixed to his clothes without setting off the store's alarm. But at any rate, your press secretary said that the man ordered a cocktail and then began playing Tetris on his Game Boy, when—and I think you, sir, repeated this in a speech you made last Friday before the AFL-CIO—you saw something crawling out of his ear and you reached over and took it between your thumb and index finger and, looking closer at it, discovered that it was a woman, a woman about the size of the letter "o" in a magazine or a newspaper. I think you even indicated a point size, but I don't have the transcript handy here. Your press secretary then went on to say that within the next forty-eight hours, you and the First Lady were married. Could you fill in some of the details about what exactly transpired in the forty-eight hours between the time that you plucked the First Lady from the ear of the man at the after-hours club and the marriage ceremony?

A: First of all, let me say this—I think it's very important that people not lose confidence in our retail industry's anti-shoplifting magnetic tag program and I have urged the business community to continue utilizing the program in order to curtail pilferage and avoid the need to pass along revenue losses to customers in the form of higher prices. Now . . . when Barbara crawled out of this fellow's ear—and I think I compared her size to that of an 8-point Times Roman lowercase "o"—I didn't know what she was. I plucked her off this guy, who said absolutely nothing and just continued playing Tetris, held her in the light, and asked her what her name was. She said Barbara and she asked me what my name was. I introduced myself and then I said that it was difficult to talk here, would she like to come back to my place. Now I think it's critical here for people to understand that this wasn't the clichéd bar pickup line it may appear to be. Because she was so tiny, it was extremely difficult to hear her, and with the jukebox blaring it was impossible. When we got home, we talked and we talked and it became apparent I think to both of us that we were just in complete synch on every level—politically, philosophically, spiritually—and it was equally apparent that we were physically quite attracted to each other. Now here's where some of the controversy's been generated and I appreciate the opportunity to clear some of this up. Sex presented some very real difficulties. I had to use a jeweler's loupe in order to find her vagina and her clitoris. Utilizing a bristle from the tiny applicator used to apply solution to micro-format audio cleaning cassettes, I jury-rigged an erotic toy which I could manipulate to give her an orgasm. She then insisted that I come, too. I told her that it didn't really matter, that just experiencing her own pleasure and passion was satisfying to me, but she insisted. And she insisted that she bring about my orgasm. She tried running up and down my penis in an effort to somehow generate enough friction to cause an orgasm but it didn't work and she was soon exhausted. After a rest, Barb came up with an ingenious suggestion. We cut a shoeshine cloth into a thin strip, glued the ends together to form a continuous loop, and rigged up an oblong treadmill. Barb ran in the center of the strip causing it to turn and I put my penis inside the end of the loop and the friction of the cloth buffing my erection soon did the trick.

Q: Mr. President, do you condone the colorization of Civil War daguerreotypes, and, if so, why?

A: I do indeed condone the colorization of Civil War daguerreotypes. I believe that if Mathew Brady had had access to color film he would have used it.

Q: Sir, you've recently urged Americans and, in particular, poor Americans to nutritionally supplement their food with their own hair and nail clippings. Could you expand on this?

A: Our nails and hair are made out of a protein called keratin. Keratin provides us with a wonderfully inexpensive way to supplement the protein content of our families' diets. Our bodies are like farms— we're growing this perfectly good source of protein right from our scalps and our fingers and our toes—and what do we do with it? We throw it away. I think that especially for parents having trouble providing their children with three square meals a day, this is an economical—and I've been assured by the Surgeon General, healthy—solution. Using an industrial grinder, you simply pulverize the clippings into a fine powder. Then you can add the powder to soups, cereals, shakes, chopped meat, whatever. By incorporating pulverized hair and nail clippings into your family's recipes, you should be able to use 25 percent less beef and still exceed the U.S. Recommended Daily Allowance for protein.

When we got back to the hotel, Arleen was still quivering with excitement.

"Oh man, what a thrill that was for me! The drama, the sensation of history in the making . . . but I don't know about grinding up my toenail clippings and mixing them into the meatloaf."

"Look, babe, we're not exactly poor," I said.

I handed her a statement from our Japanese licensing company that my agent had faxed to the hotel. It showed bottom-line quarterly revenues for Team Leyner from the My Cousin, My Gastroenterologist Miniature Golf Course in Yokohama of over 68,000,000 yen.

Up in our suite, I splashed cold water on my face, slicked my hair back, slapped on some Versace Eau de Toilette, pocketed my gloves and lock picks, affixed my six-and-a-half-inch stainless steel Gerber survival knife in a Cordura sheath to a tie-down on my right leg, and holstered my SIG P-226 9-mm pistol loaded with 15 rounds of ARMCO 115-grain full-metal-jacketed military spec ammo to my left leg. Arleen had zapped the TV to life and was mimicking an aerobics instructor who was firming fanny on a beach on Maui.

"Arleen, I'm going to the National Museum of Health and Medicine. Do you want to come?"

"Nah. I think I'm going to take a nap for a while. Will you be long?"

"I hope not, babe."

I managed a glancing kiss as she slithered back and forth across the carpet in response to the rhythmic exhortations of the television.

I was back with the vial of Lincoln's morning breath in less than an hour. Security at the National Museum of Health and Medicine was a joke. The vial wasn't under guard; it wasn't monitored by surveillance cameras; it wasn't even kept in a locked vitrine. It was propped up on a table in the middle of an empty room.

"What do you think of this?" I asked Arleen, handing her the vial.

Arleen shrugged.

"Arleen, what you've got in your hand happens to be a vial of fucking Abraham Lincoln's morning breath. And it's my pleasure and honor as your husband to invite you to join me in partaking of a snort or two."

Arleen looked at the vial.

She looked at me.

She looked back at the vial.

And then back at me.

"Let's get stoned," she said.

It's impossible to do justice to the smell in words. One may try to quicken the olfactory imagination with poetic evocations like "suppurating abscess . . . colonic effluvia . . . smegma." But nothing comes close to capturing the overwhelming stench that wafted from the vial when I removed its rubber stopper. It's suspected that Lincoln was afflicted with an inherited disease called Marfan syndrome. Perhaps this accounts for the unbelievable foulness of his morning breath. Unfortunately, the vial was not dated. We only know that it was prepared during the Lincoln presidency. Halitologists contend that anxiety and tension can affect the odor of one's breath. Perhaps the sample was taken in 1863, the morning after the Battle of Chancellorsville, when Union forces commanded by Joseph Hooker were decimated by the Confederate troops of Stonewall Jackson and Robert E. Lee. Or perhaps Lincoln had simply split a sopressata and smoked mozzarella sub with hot peppers and extra onions with Mary Todd the night before the sample was collected.

But did we get high? you ask.

CHAPTER FOUR

The psychoactive effect of Lincoln's morning breath was quite as astonishing as its aroma.

I could easily devote the balance of this memoir in its entirety to detailing the 12-hour psychedelic joyride/Götterdämmerung that Arleen and I experienced under the influence of the rancid vapor. But highlights shall suffice.

Sex was intense. Creamy lime cum. Then creamy apricot cum. Then a mint gel. And finally a cyan-yellow-magenta swirl that actually burst into flame. Now, I'm no stranger to chemically enhanced lovemaking. For instance, I've explored the romantic possibilities of the anabolic steroid Oral-Turinabol (OT), used in conjunction with Piracetam, a drug which increases endurance and enhances concentration. I've been known to revive a humdrum evening with a discreet injection of recombinant erythropoietin (rEPO), which raises the red blood-cell count so that more oxygen is carried through the circulatory system, for big performance gains. And every so often, I like to turn the lights down low, put something lush and dreamy on the stereo, and inject myself with blood plasma from hibernating woodchucks, which imparts to the lovemaking an extraordinarily serene and sylvan quality. But these paled in comparison to Lincoln's morning breath.

Using a piece of charcoal and a sheet of hotel stationery, Arleen did a rubbing of the welter of protuberant veins on my biceps. Had the neuronal networks linking the left and right sides of our brains not undergone an amazing spurt of spontaneous hyperplasia as a result of our inhaling the gaseous relic of the Great Emancipator, surely the rubbing would not have achieved the mystical profundity that it held for us that afternoon. With Arleen's permission (of course), I quote verbatim from her journal entry dated April 12, 1991: "We gazed at the rubbing for over an hour in awed silence. Like the intricate tesselations that decorate the walls and floors of the Alhambra, the veins on Mark's biceps bespeak a cosmic meta-mind, a universal and primordial mentality of form, the interplay of energy and entropy that preceded life and will follow it. I will never be able to look at his biceps again without a sense of epiphany."

Do you know the commercial where the heavily mustached old woman in a black shroud drinks strawberry Nestlé's Quik and turns into this buxom bombshell in pasties and G-string, and she squats down for a second in a mud puddle, and when she gets up, her buttocks are covered with leeches, and Jesus appears holding a Barbie, and two beams of sparkling particles shoot from the eyes of the Barbie and vaporize the leeches, and the bombshell gets on her motorcycle, and pink florets of exhaust spurt from its tailpipe spelling out the words *Be All That You Can Be*? Try watching that on Lincoln's morning breath. It's un-fucking-believable.

How about the scene from *On Golden Pond* where Jane Fonda arrives from Omega Centauri to "visit" her father in the nursing home? You remember what it was like to watch her tenderly remove his toupee and then his hearing aid and his bifocals and his dentures and his truss, and then suddenly drain his cerebrospinal fluid through that horrible sucking proboscis? Well, imagine what it's like watching that scene on Lincoln's morning breath. It's almost unbearable. But would you believe that the two of us were actually jumping up and down on the bed, cheering?

It was midnight. Arleen danced on the balcony clad only in white stretch-vinyl jeans and Walkman, bathed in moonlight. I'd been cooling out in the tub—the small fondue forks from my Swiss Army knife vibrating slightly in various acupuncture points on my physique. I focused my video camera beyond Arleen, and scanned the revamped cityscape. Every federal building—White House, Capitol, Executive and Congressional offices, Departments of State, Justice, Commerce, etc.—had been razed and rebuilt in an astonishing new style, each designed and constructed to simulate building blocks toppled in a toddler's tantrum. And looming over the city, dramatically illuminated by floodlights, was a huge 1,000-foot white marble baby in diapers, arms akimbo, smugly admiring his own vandalism. The Überkind.

I twanged each impaled fondue fork and zoomed in on the monolithic tot's chubby smirk.

"Überkind, Überkind, a thousand feet tall, what's the best diet cola of them all?"

"Diet Pepsi. Diet Pepsi #1."

(I was reading the Überkind's marble lips through the zoom lens of my camcorder.)

"Thanks, babe," I said, passing out.

In *The Decline and Fall of the Roman Empire,* Ed Gibbon's gossipy tell-all chronicle of the West's first millennium, Attila returns to his wooden palace beyond the Danube after sacking Aquileia, an Italian maritime city on the Adriatic coast, and declaims: "Sure we enriched ourselves with the spoils of a wealthy and effeminate people. Sure we stole their gold and jewels. Sure we stripped their palaces of splendid and costly furniture. We wantonly destroyed exquisite works of art. We defiled consecrated objects. We tortured and slaughtered their clergy. And let no man say that we did not imbibe tremendous quantities of Falernian wine and slake our sensual appetites on helpless, trembling captives—male and female. And yet, notwithstanding the amazing amount of fun I had in Aquileia, it's so great to be home. My home . . . Here I don't worry every minute about having to be the epitome of rapacious avarice and unrelenting cruelty. I can relax and be myself. How sweet to be in my large wooden palace again. How sweet to lie again in the warm beds of my innumerable wives."

Could it be pure coincidence that the sentiments of one of history's luminary strongmen and belletrists so perfectly mirror those of another who lives almost sixteen centuries later? I felt *exactly* the same way about returning home. Sure D.C. had been a blast. Sure the Lincoln's morning breath had been primo shit. But it just felt so damn good to be back at headquarters.

And, as usual, the staff made quite a to-do over my homecoming. For the occasion, Desiree had outfitted the full detachment of bionic elderly bodyguards in the resplendent regalia of Hungarian hussars. Imagine: rimming the promenade that leads to the front entrance of Team Leyner HQ, a double column of testosterone-enhanced 90-year-old women with electrically activated polymer musculature in fur busbies with plumes and vivid yellow busby bags, sky blue dolman jackets, fur-lined pelisses slung over the shoulder, tight braided red trousers, and concertina-crinkled boots. Was I absolutely, 100 percent on-the-money when I hired Desiree Buttcake or what? I mean the woman just has this flair, this terrific panache about everything she does.

Frequently when I return from a tour or an extended holiday, the media is invited on the grounds to cover the festivities. But Baby Lago, my doe-eyed press attaché, had decided to keep this homecoming private. Ergo the huge banner depicting a just-awakened Honest Abe sitting up in bed and yawning, as his hapless valet succumbs and crumples to the floor.

*   *   *

With Shalimar snapping at our heels (Baby Lago's three Lhasa apsos are each named after a classic fragrance by Guerlain: Shalimar, Samsara, and Mitsouko), we strode through the ebullient corridors of the new office annex, acknowledging the fervent salutations of word processors, proofreaders, and mailroom clerks as we headed toward the executive conference gallery, an elegantly appointed suite of terrazzo and aquamarine bulletproof glass.

Immediately upon returning from a trip, I convene a meeting of my inner circle to assess the current status of Team Leyner projects and to discuss opportunities or problems that may have arisen in my absence. Either Joe Casale or Desiree Buttcake will have prepared an agenda of matters they consider urgent and I'll have usually punched a dozen or so items into my laptop while on the plane or in the limo. Do I always conduct my business with this kind of nonstop indefatigable intensity and zeal? You bet I do. Do I make any distinction whatsoever between my personal life and my career? No, sir, I do not. I work and I play at one speed: hyperdrive—Mach 9, adrenaline OD, total warp. It's the only way I know how to live.

We get letters from kids all over the world asking everything from "What's your favorite font?" to "How many egg whites do you eat a day?" But you'd be surprised at how many young people write in with the same basic question: "How do I know if I'm great or if I'm the victim of megalomaniacal delusions?" My standard reply is: "Sorry, kid, you're probably the victim of megalomaniacal delusions because only an infinitesimal percentage of the species is truly destined for greatness." Since I was a small child, I've had the feeling that simply by clenching my jaw and visualizing an explosion, I could blow up planets or stars in galaxies thousands of light-years from earth. Megalomaniacal delusion or fact? I've been lucky enough over the past few years to have developed a very close friendship with the acclaimed theoretical physicist Stephen Hawking. I first became personally acquainted with Stephen when his secretary wrote a letter to my editor at Harmony Books, to say that Hawking didn't feel completely comfortable publishing *A Brief History of Time* until I'd reviewed the book's fundamental theorem and given my critical imprimatur. Luckily I was between projects and happy to oblige Stephen and his publisher, Bantam Books. Recently, I was seated ringside next to Stephen at the Evander Holyfield/George Foreman bout in Atlantic City, and I mentioned my suspicion that I had the ability to destroy celestial bodies simply by willing it, and not only did Stephen find this plausible in the abstract, but actually correlated it with several heretofore unexplained supernovae.

I brought my fist down on the conference room table with peremptory authority.

"Let's get busy, folks. Joe, what do you have for me, babe?"

"Well, first of all, Mr. Leyner, Ken Dietrich—he's VP Marketing for Pepsico Inc.—called about the agreement wherein you mention Diet Pepsi in a new book and Pepsico remunerates Team Leyner with $750,000 in cash, plus $250,000 in stock. He basically wants to know if we've made any progress on the product insert."

"Tell Dietrich it's done, not to worry about it anymore, and to get the check in the mail. What else?"

"Mr. Leyner, we have a minor personnel problem. Y'know our regulation prohibiting any Team Leyner employee from earning income outside the organization? Well, one of the mailroom clerks is selling marijuana grown on pieces of sod he's removed from various major league baseball stadiums. He's got Wrigley Wiggly, Fenway Dream Bean, Comiskey Park and Ride . . . he's even selling marijuana grown on stadium sod from vintage years, like 1969 Shea Stadium Sinsemilla. I didn't want to make a decision about the guy until you got back."

"Eighty-six him, babe. No freelancing means no freelancing, no exceptions. And impound the sod."

"OK, Mr. Leyner."

"Joe, any paternity suits this week?"

"Only two, Mr. Leyner. Both women are members of the Ecuadorian Olympic Equestrian Team, and their attorney's hired a forensic DNA-fingerprinting laboratory to provide incontestable evidence that you're the father."

"As soon as the meeting's over, Joe, I want you to Fed Ex the director of the lab a Team Leyner belt buckle and insignia magnet, and an official Team Leyner trivet. OK, babe?"

"Consider it done, Mr. Leyner."

"Anything else, Joe?"

"Two more things. While you were away, a Japanese industrialist named Takeshi Oshiro, who owns the Uchiyama Paper Manufacturing Company, paid $19,250 in a public auction at Sotheby's for one of your discarded deodorant sticks with a stray armpit hair and—this is such a weird coincidence—he's hired the same DNA-fingerprinting lab to confirm that it's your armpit hair, and if it's not, Sotheby's has agreed to refund the 19K and change. And lastly, I just wanted to remind you that this coming Friday they're shooting the commercial for Becker Surgical Devices and they need you on the set at about ten A.M."

"Thanks, Joe, good job. Desiree, you're up."

"Well, first of all, I'm happy to report that we're close to completing a comprehensive demographic analysis of your readership, which means that now we'll be able to develop software that can alter your texts depending on which regional or even local audiences we're targeting. For instance, in a forthcoming novel, you have a giant who eats postmenopausal crossing guards. OK—we now know that you have a rabidly enthusiastic following in the rural northwest, but in the rural northwest they don't have crossing guards because generally kids out there don't walk to school. So with the new demographically based software, the computer can flag something like that and change the postmenopausal crossing guards to postmenopausal school-bus drivers or whatever is appropriate for the rural northwest edition. It's yet another way of making readers feel as if you're writing just for them."

"That's really cool."

"It's also a pleasure to report that the initial response to the 1-800-T-LEYNER number has been just fabulous."

"What's the deal on that, Dez? You get a choice of different messages when you call or what?"

"A fan calls 1-800-T-LEYNER and—using a touch-tone phone, of course—dials 1 to hear an excerpt from your upcoming book, 2 for your most intimate thoughts about weight-lifting, 3 for dating advice, 4 for an up-close-and-personal tidbit from Arleen, and 5 for a cute anecdote about Carmella. And the messages change every week. It's $2 for the first minute, $1 for every additional minute. Fans under 18, please don't call without your parents' permission."

"Excellent stuff, Desiree."

"Mark, based on the notes that you made before you left for D.C., we've worked up a draft of the press release you want put out, and I just want to make sure that we're all in synch here. You basically want to inform book critics that, in the event of a bad review, Team Leyner will not be held responsible for the wrath of fans who see you as the articulator of their vision and who see your detractors as a threat to their way of life. Consequently, Team Leyner cannot be held responsible for the physical safety of the reviewer and his or her family, in the event of an unfavorable notice. Is that about the gist of it?"

"That's it exactly."

"And you want this put out in general release?"

"I want this sent directly to our *friends* themselves—to the Lehmann-Haupts and the Kakutanis, to the Yardleys, to the Wolcotts and the Atlases and the Raffertys . . . understood?"

"Understood."

"I want everyone here to remember something. Team Leyner plays hardball. If anyone—and I don't care who it is, I don't care if it's my own grandmother—if anyone attempts to impede the fulfillment of our destiny, we fuck with them big time."

"We fuck with them big time," everyone chorused.

"Anything else, Dez?"

"This is somewhat of a corollary to what we've just been discussing. Joe and I have been analyzing a trend we see developing in media coverage of Team Leyner, and we've come up with a means of countering what we perceive as an incipient problem that could become dangerous unless we act decisively now. There are, increasingly, those in the media who would twist the work we're doing in our writers' vocational counseling intensives into something sinister. Scurrilous rumors abound about your supposed steroid use, your messianic fantasies, your weakness for Hispanic women . . . Joe and I propose a public relations program designed to resuscitate your image in the media. We propose that you engage in a well-publicized personal campaign to help agoraphobic housewives with their poetry. We see two options here: video teleconferencing, which enables you to counsel agoraphobic poetesses wherever they live without having to leave headquarters—signals are relayed through a satellite over the Yukon to a ground station in northern Michigan, to a satellite over the West Indies and finally to a fiber-optic link in Atlanta. Or you can simply visit the women at their homes. What do you think?"

"I think I'll make housecalls."

"You like the proposal?"

"Desiree, Joe—it's top-notch work. I'm proud of you both."

"Thanks, Mark."

"Thanks, Mr. Leyner."

"Baby Lago, why don't we finish up with your concert report."

"OK. Well, we have Libidinal Hegemony at Maxwell's tonight. And tomorrow night at CBGB's, there's Fried Wind and

Dick Cheez. And all three bands are comping you and anyone from Team Leyner who wants to go."

"Thanks, sweetie. Folks, it's getting late. I'm sure you're all tired. So I'd like to just say good night, thanks again for all the hard work you're doing, and . . . it's great to be back."

"Mr. Leyner . . ."

"Yes, Joe?"

"Mr. Leyner, do you have a few minutes? There's something kinda private I'd like to talk to you about."

"Sure, babe. Why don't you meet me at The Triggerman in about ten minutes. We'll have a few drinks and talk."

The Triggerman is a bar/pistol range that we opened for Team Leyner staffers so that, at the end of a long day, there'd be a place "on-campus" where they could have a few drinks and shoot firearms—a place for them to blow off steam. I like to come down to The Triggerman after a late night meeting to unwind and maybe chat with some of the lower-echelon employees with whom I don't normally interact.

I'd just emptied a magazine of 125-grain jacketed hollowpoints from my six-and-a-half-inch .44 Auto Mag, when I noticed Joe on the bar stool next to mine.

"Mr. Leyner, I'm in love."

"Hold on a second, Joe," I said, removing my ear protectors. "You're what?"

"I'm in love."

I ordered two triple Chivases and another fifteen rounds of hollowpoints.

"In love with whom, babe?"

"Mr. Leyner, I'm in love with Desiree. Y'know, we've been working really closely together on that press release for the book critics and on the PR program and . . . I just fell totally in love with her. And the trouble is that I know she doesn't feel the same way about me. I mean she's such an incredibly beautiful woman, and I . . . well, I'm not trying to be self-deprecating, but I'm not like traditionally handsome. And this unrequited stuff makes me feel like a bit of an A-hole."

Joe will not say the word *asshole.* He says, instead, "A-hole." Similarly, he will not utter the epithet *douche-bag,* preferring the more delicate "D-bag." "Go develop E of the S, you FS-munching MG-head" is "Go develop elephantiasis of the scrotum, you foreskin-munching Merv Griffin-head"—invective overheard when a careless tailor accidentally pinned one of Joe's flippers to his inseam while fitting him for a Team Leyner softball uniform.

"Look, Joe, there are all kinds of women, and I truly believe that there's someone out there for everyone. Just take a look at some of these personal ads here." I reached across the bar for the newspaper. "For example, look at this one: 'Do you wear peasant blouses and billowy gypsy skirts? I'm a drooling, catheterized, cataract-eyed white supremacist from Baton Rouge who has three to four lucid hours a day. Let's go underground where Zionist water-fluoridators and Russian space debris can't find us.' What do you want to bet that this guy gets a couple of hundred responses?"

"Well, I'm not interested in other women. I'm interested in Desiree."

"Joe, check this out," I said, handing him my first target, which had just arrived at the bar. I'd managed to achieve, at a range of 50 yards, a four-inch seven-round group on the black of the target, with most of the shots less than two inches apart. "Not bad, huh?"

"Really great, Mr. Leyner," Joe said morosely.

"C'mon, Joe, lighten up, would ya? Maybe there's a way for you to somehow provoke Dez into feeling romantic about you."

"Provoke her how?"

"Well, I can only tell you what works for me, babe. I take my clothes off. Women go nuts. I know that sounds stupid, but it's how I do it that's important—it's the style, it's the head trip I get into. Each item of clothing—leather blazer, T-shirt, snake-skin boots, jeans, socks, and finally underpants—is removed as if I were stripping for an audience at a maximum security prison for criminally insane women. With that masturbatory simultaneity of languor and urgency, I whip the floor with my silk bikini briefs that have been stretched grotesquely out of shape after a day of restraining my restless genitals, and I hear—in my head—the horrific cacophony of gasps, moans, ululations, stomping feet, shrieks, sobs, pleas . . . y'know what I'm saying?"

"I guess so, Mr. Leyner, but I don't know if I could—"

"Listen, the thing you've got to be careful about is the effect something like that can have on a woman. I was with this notary public Felice Ruiz once, and I'm doing the whole bit and I get to the part where I'm whipping the floor with my silk undies, and I guess my body's just too much for the poor girl—she goes apoplectic on me. She's hyperventilating, taking in giant gulps of air, foaming at the mouth. Then she's purple in the face, clutching at her throat, clutching at her chest, like she's having some kind of seizure. She falls to the ground and, writhing, manages to point to a cabinet in the armoire. I rush to the cabinet, open it, and there are two bottles, gin and vodka. I make a split-second decision—vodka. I bring the bottle to Felice, who's rolling on the ground, tearing at her hair. I show her the vodka bottle. She shakes her head violently back and forth, kicking her feet. I rush back to the armoire and retrieve the bottle of gin. Felice is trying to say something, and I put my ear to her lips, but her mumbling and grunting are completely unintelligible. I quickly produce a pad and a pen. Can you write? I ask. She nods, and I hand her the writing implements. Her body jerking spasmodically, she manages to scrawl: Singapore Sling. Now, a Singapore Sling is a fairly elaborate cocktail; it involves shaking together gin, cherry brandy, lemon juice, and powdered sugar, pouring it into a tall glass filled with ice and topping it with soda water. But I concoct the drink as rapidly as I can, bring it to the convulsant Felice, tilt the highball glass to her lips, and let her drink. After a few sips, her paroxysms begin to subside, and she's eventually able to return to the sofa. So what I'm trying to say is that you have to exercise some degree of caution here . . . are you following me, babe?"

"Yes, Mr. Leyner."

"Joe, can I get you another drink?"

"No thanks, Mr. Leyner, I think I should get to bed. I've got a pretty full schedule in the morning."

"OK, babe. Sweet dreams. And thanks again for all your effort."

I love that guy.

I ordered an anisette with three spent shells. The shells, still muzzle-hot, warm the anisette for a nice nightcap.

I felt good.

The first applicant whom we accepted for the agoraphobic housewife-poet program was Mary Elizabeth Thuring, whose manuscript *Coarse-Cut Marmalade Enema Binge* opened with the erotic sonnet "The Wilted Crudités."

Eyeballs stew in hot sockets
During long sexual dream of bearded
Blacksmith in crotchless high-bib overalls
Hammering hot metal on an anvil.
Funny . . . isn't this Belmar?
I lie ungarnished in the sand,
Sweet carrion for beach hyenas.

The plaited strands of his licorice noose
Become sticky in the heat of the sun.
Soon thousands of flies form a buzzing black garland
Around the neck of the condemned candy cowboy.
Yes, Emily Dickinson,
Once I did love a Pakistani badminton champion.
You got a problem with that?

I spent some six-and-a-half hours with Mary at her lovely home, poring over her manuscript, rearranging the order of the poems for maximum effect, suggesting various emendations and deletions (for example, I cut the following two lines: "Whiskey-swilling itinerant beauticians/Wax the bikini line of Isis" from the first stanza of "The Wilted Crudités").

When I return to Team Leyner HQ from Mary Elizabeth Thuring's home, it's approximately 5:20 A.M.

Arleen is being led out the front door, her wrists handcuffed behind her, surrounded by FBI agents. A miscellany of Team Leyner employees is milling around, smoking cigarettes, muttering, glaring, cursing. Joe Casale is screaming at the top of his lungs one of his cryptic algebraic curses: "Go MW your PGs, you pimply D'ed, CL-flapping, U-quaffing YIs!" My immediate chain of thought is: missing fiction workshop participants . . . federal kidnapping indictments . . . prison.

I throw one of the agents—a burly guy about 6′ 6″, 275 pounds—up against a column and slap him hard across the face about a dozen times.

His playmates draw their weapons.

"You gonna shoot me, you motherfuckin' morons? There'd be riots in every major city of this country!"

"Holster your weapons, men," orders the senior agent. "Holster your weapons!"

"That's better," I snarl. "Now, what's the fucking problem here?"

"Mark Leyner and Arleen Portada, you are both being charged with theft of a federally protected bio-historical specimen."

Ahhhh, I thought to myself, greatly relieved, this has nothing to do with kidnapping fiction workshop participants, it's the Lincoln's morning breath. It's just a bullshit larceny rap.

"Joe, get Gary Knobloch [chief corporate counsel for Team Leyner] over here right away—OK, babe. The rest of you get back to work. Everything's going to be all right."

*   *   *

Knobloch was leafing through the U.S. Criminal Code.

"Let's see . . . Tailgating a Presidential Motorcade . . . Talking Dirty to a Congressional Page . . . Terrorizing a U.S. Mail Carrier . . . Testifying Falsely Against a Fetus . . . ah, here we go. Theft of a Federally Protected Bio-Historical Specimen. First offense: Weekly punitive confiscation. Second offense: Removal of the nasal septum, leaving offender with one large nostril. Third offense: Underwater spear-gun execution by scuba-diving firing squad. Listen, Mark, I don't like telling you what to do—you're my favorite writer, you're my favorite client, you're the godfather of my two children—but I strongly advise you to plead guilty on this thing and live with punitive confiscation once a week. If we go to trial and there's any way they can prove that you did something like this before, you could be walking around with one big hole in the middle of your face. Wouldn't make a very attractive book jacket photo, kid."

"Arleen, Joe, Dez . . . what do you think?" I asked.

"I agree, Mr. Leyner," Joe said. "One big nostril wouldn't look that great on a book cover . . . but I guess I'm not really one to talk."

"Thanks, babe, but I meant what do you think about copping a guilty plea?"

"I agree with Gary," Desiree said. "I think you guys should play it safe. And you have so much stuff—maybe losing something once a week would be a blessing in disguise, sort of like spring cleaning."

"Arleen?"

"Yeah, I guess so . . . but I don't know why I'm even being charged. It wasn't my idea to steal that shit."

"Oh, like you said, 'Mark, it's so wrong, take the Lincoln's morning breath back to the National Museum of Health and Medicine this minute.' "

"I didn't say I said that."

"And like you didn't get off on it as much as I did."

"I never said I didn't get off on it, you creep."

"Hey, you two, c'mon. So we plead guilty to First-Offense Theft of a Federally Protected Bio-Historical Specimen and accept weekly punitive confiscation—yes?"

"Yes, Gary."

The punishment consisted of having one item confiscated each week. At 10 A.M. every Monday morning, the authorities would arrive in a large truck. They'd read the statement that the courts required them to read prior to each punitive confiscation, they'd handcuff us, and they'd put us in the truck in a special enclosed compartment, where we were strapped to chairs in front of a 27-inch television screen. The identical 30-minute video was shown to us each week. And while we were watching the video—a porno film with all the sex edited out, leaving only the wooden narrative segues—the one item was confiscated and placed in the truck's main compartment. (The Supreme Court has since ruled that forcing someone to view only the narrative segues from a pornographic film is in violation of the Eighth Amendment.) We were then allowed to return to our home. We were never told which item was confiscated. Sometimes it was obvious: the piano, the living room sofa, the wall phone in the kitchen, etc. But often we wouldn't know what was taken until we needed it and it wasn't there. For instance, one morning I badly needed my styptic pencil. (I groom myself with the same manic intensity with which I do everything else, and often after I shave, it looks as if I've gone face-first through an automobile windshield.) I looked in the drawer and the styptic pencil was gone—confiscated. Then one evening I was making pesto sauce, and I opened the cabinet to get the pignoli nuts and they were gone—confiscated. And one night we were making love, and

Arleen went into the bathroom to get her tube of prescription maximum-strength spermicide (my spermatozoa are exceptionally robust and have developed a total resistance to over-the-counter spermicides) and the tube was gone—confiscated. We were prohibited from replacing confiscated items. If we were discovered to have replaced a confiscated item, our punitive status would be upgraded to second offense—nasal septumectomy.

"**S**ir, is there anywhere in particular you want to go?"

"No, just keep flying."

I'm in the XXT7, a top-secret, experimental hyperspeed jet fighter that does about Mach 8. I just had to get away from it all, get up in the azure void of high-altitude airspace for a while, try to get some perspective.

"Well, sir, how about this: I'll swing west across the Indonesian archipelago, cut northwest across the Bay of Bengal, take her due west over India, Pakistan, Iran, the Persian Gulf, Saudi Arabia, north over Syria and Turkey, the Black Sea, we'll follow the Dnieper River from Kiev to Moscow, cut over toward St. Petersburg, cross the Baltic, Sweden, Norway, then swing sharply to the east, transverse the Arctic Ocean, follow the Bering Straits east, cross the Bering Sea, and head south over the Pacific past the eastern coast of Japan toward the Philippines and I can have you back in Malaysia by suppertime."

I don't even really hear what the pilot's saying, so I just nod. "Yeah, yeah, that's fine, that's great."

Y'know, when I was a teenager, I was told that I'd spend my entire life in and out of institutions, pathologically maladapted, living on society's fringes . . . well, it didn't turn out quite that way, folks. I'm only 36 years old; I've achieved international notoriety as a best-selling author, body builder, martial artist; I make more in a year from product endorsements than most people make in a lifetime; I've got a multimillion-dollar headquarters

with a guard tower, gatehouses, patrol dogs, armed sentries, a vast
warren of underground tunnels; I've got a gorgeous wife and an
entourage of gofers and sycophants . . . So what's the problem,
right? The problem is that when you reach a level of achievement
that few people have ever reached, when you routinely do things
that no one else is even capable of imagining never mind attempting, when you are destined for greatness and possess the fortitude
and inner focus to fulfill that destiny . . . you have no real friends,
no real family. People look at you with awe, with fear, with lust,
with suspicion, with envy . . . but not with affection. This is just
a fact of life for me. It's just the way it is. So is it paranoia or
my fierce instinct for survival that makes me suspect an agent pro-
vocateur in our midst? How did Iron Man Wang's hit squad of
horny robo-trash find me so easily that day on the interstate outside of Wenton's Mill? Why did Rocco Trezza suddenly disappear?
Is it pure coincidence that the same DNA-fingerprinting laboratory retained by the attorney for both members of the Ecuadorian
Olympic Equestrian Team is also analyzing my armpit hair
for Sotheby's? How did the FBI connect me to the Lincoln's morning breath heist? Here's an even better question: Why does the
possibility that there's a traitor in my inner circle excite me so
much?

There was a full moon. We took our clothes off and carefully
folded them over the branches of a tree that jutted obliquely from
the sand dune. We waded out into the sea and started to swim
toward Kana Island, where the abandoned insane asylum rose in the
white moonlight. She swam effortlessly, smiling, humming jingles.
    "I didn't catch your name," I said, adjusting the speedometer on
my diving watch to see how many knots I could do on my back.
    "My name is Patty Amato," she replied.
    "What hotel are you staying at?"
    "The Hilton at Sugar Plantation. How about you?"

"I'm at the Green Isle . . . it's sort of out-of-town. It's full of rats, but it's cheap."

"The Hilton's beautiful—really service oriented."

With that, she arched her back and submerged, curving 180 degrees to the sea floor and then 180 degrees back to the surface at my side.

"Do you know what this is?" she asked, handing me a small cylindrical object that she'd plucked from the bottom.

I studied it for a moment. "It's called 'awakura.' It's the felt-tipped reproductive organ of a certain bioluminescent crustacean. Do you like sushi?"

"Yeah . . . why?"

"Well, you can eat that. It's considered quite a delicacy in Japan. And it's very expensive. In fact, in Tokyo, the difference between sushi regular and sushi deluxe is usually that the sushi deluxe includes awakura and the sushi regular doesn't."

"What about this thing at the end here? Do they eat that?"

"That's felt. You just spit that out."

She ate it and spit the end back into the sea.

"Oh, I forgot to tell you," I said, winking, "it's a powerful aphrodisiac."

She looked at me with raised eyebrows and I started to laugh.

"That whole thing was bullshit, wasn't it . . . there's no such thing as awakura. Right?"

I couldn't stop laughing.

She put me in a hammerlock and held my head underwater.

"Right?" she repeated.

Bubbles of laughter clustered at the surface.

She let me go.

"I'm sorry," I gasped. "Friends? C'mon . . . friends for life?"

She was laughing now herself.

"You're a fucking dickhead, y'know that? What did I just eat anyway?"

"Can't say, Patricia . . . hey, look, we're almost at the island."

"Yeah, just a little more. Do you have those pay movies in your room?"

"We don't even have television sets. I'm telling you, the Green Isle is no-frills."

"Well, last night there was a really cool movie—it was called *Miracle Worker 2200*. It's like a remake of *The Miracle Worker*, but it takes place in the year 2200 and Anne Sullivan implants all these electronic microprosthetic devices into Helen Keller, like this infra-red sensor to pick up hot spots—y'know, heat sources—and this voice synthesizer so that she can sound like anything she wants to—y'know, like a flute or an electric piano or an Australian dingo or anything. Y'know, it's so amazing when you think about what science can do."

We had reached the shore . . . Kana Island. Before it was con-demned by the government, its medieval insane asylum was consid-ered a true house of horrors. There were persistent reports of torture, cannibalism, human sacrifice, and bizarre medical experimentation. As we emerged from the water, we observed each other's nakedness in the moonlight and we embraced.

"Do you get collagen injections or are those your real lips?" I asked her.

"Are you serious?"

For the first time that night, I had the feeling that she thought there was something wrong with me.

We walked up the road to the asylum and entered through its huge gates of rusted iron.

As soon as we got into the building, we could hear the rats, thousands of them, their scampering claws reverberating through the empty wards.

"Let's go right to the warden's quarters—they're on the top floor. Can you walk up twenty flights? Can you walk up twenty flights in an insane asylum . . . *naked*?" I asked.

She gave me that look again.

"What's the difference? Twenty flights are twenty flights, naked or clothed. What's wrong with you?"

We climbed to the top floor of the asylum. There was a utility room across from the stairway. We walked in and I strode directly to the refrigerator and opened it.

"Look, Patricia," I said, pointing to a harmonica in the freezer.

She took it in her hands. And she put her full lips on the ice-cold harmonica and she blew. A plaintive arpeggio echoed throughout the building and thousands of rats began making their way toward the top floor.

"You knew exactly where that refrigerator was . . . how did you know that?" Patricia asked me, trembling.

I put my arm around her shoulder and led her to the warden's quarters.

"Patricia, look."

I pointed to a crudely lettered sign above the door.

It said, *"Green Isle."*

She began screaming.

And so did I.

"Oh wow, Mark, that was great! And it was so spooky the way you read it!"

"I'm really glad you liked it, Baby Lago. It's called 'The Warden of Green Isle' by Imelda Kabakow, one of the premier genre-restricted authors in North America. I hope it doesn't give you nightmares."

"Oh, I love nightmares!"

"Listen, it's late, and I have to be up pretty early in the morning."

"Oh yeah, they're filming that commercial tomorrow, right?"

"Yeah. Baby Lago, I wanted to thank you for all the work you did in Tokyo negotiating the lease on that 500-story supersky-scraper headquarters for Team Leyner Nippon. You did a great job."

"It was fun!"

I bowed.

"Good night, Baby Lago-san."

"I guess you could say that I like things 'natural.' By 'natural' I mean 'naturally selected' as in Darwin, i.e., organisms with advantageous mutations are likely to outcompete the original forms, gradually outnumbering and replacing them in the population . . . that sort of thing. Sure I have my tender moments—I like the silent white dawn after a night's heavy snowfall, sometimes I like to say something sarcastic to the person making my submarine sandwich or to the person slicing meat for my gyro just to see them smile—maybe it's their first smile of the day—but basically I'm pretty contemptuous of people, because most people are weak and I find weakness pretty sickening. I like my men, my women, my coffee, my cocktails—I guess everything in my life—STRONG. That's why I can offer my unequivocal endorsement of Armor-Guard High Security Barbed Wire Fences. The choice of maximum security institutions across the country, Armor-Guard fences feature substantially longer barbs with additional barb points for superior intimidation and entanglement capabilities—"

"Cut! Cut! Hold it, Mr. Leyner."

"What's the problem?"

"We're getting a weird glare off that section of barbed wire over there . . . why don't we take a break and we'll adjust the lighting over there."

"OK, babe."

"**H**i, I'm Mark Leyner. With my reputation as a tough guy and best-selling author, I'm asked to do commercials—well, as you just saw—for all kinds of 'tough' products like penal fencing, cattle prods, bulletproof vests, etc. But when it comes to my family and my friends and my fans—those I cherish most dearly—I can be a real 'softie.' That's why when Becker Surgical Devices asked me to tell people about their balloon angioplasty equipment, I said I'd love to. There's nothing good about 'tough' stenosed arteries. When plaque accumulates, inhibiting the flow of blood to vital organs, the life of someone you love, perhaps even your own life, may be threatened. And I don't know about you, but I love life.

"Some people are preoccupied with the symbolism of their dreams and with who they might have been in past incarnations and with where their souls are going after they die, but I never think about any of that shit. I just love this earth. I love the morning. When the first morning light hits my eye, I feel like a new appliance that's been unpacked and plugged in for the first time. But my life is beautiful. Perhaps that's why I love the morning light. I have money. I have a voluptuous wife. And I have fans. People who have ugly lives often hate the morning; it means the beginning of all the pain and the toil and the flash-backs all over again, and they try to bear the unbearable until twilight, which comes on slowly with the physical sensation of a warm barbiturate liquid, and of course the black silent night—phone off the hook, doors bolted—is the full-blown anodyne. That's the circadian saga of the ugly life, in brief. When I awaken, I go outside naked. The sun—the perpetual hydrogen bomb—is my shower, and it galvanizes me, it freaks me out. A pirouetting monster emitting guttural expressions of ecstasy in the radiance of the sun . . .

"What's a typical day like for me?

"It's the late afternoon, a married woman in her forties pours the heavy syrup from a can of peaches over her breasts and looks at me. I'm sitting on a chair across the room, critiquing her masochistic poetry. When I say good-bye to her later, it's night. Under her hot halogen lamp, oil oozes from the pores of her 'T-zone.'

" 'Why wouldn't you fuck me?' she asks.

" 'I'm married. And I don't fuck the women I counsel. You asked me to take my clothes off so that you could see my body and I did that. Why don't you fuck your husband when he gets home?'

" 'He's not coming home tonight and if he was I wouldn't fuck him. I'm too angry to fuck him.'

" 'What are you angry at him about?'

" 'He's cheating on me. It's in the poems. Couldn't you figure that out?'

"I shrugged and started putting my clothes back on.

" 'How'd you get that scar over your right nipple?'

" 'I had an Uncle Jack. He was my mentor; he taught me to be a writer and to be a man. He said that when you write you march through the reader's mind like Sherman marching to the sea and you burn every neuron and synapse as you go. He taught me a secret style of Kung Fu that's based on ballroom dancing steps—the Foxtrot, Lindy, Waltz, etc.—but that's lethal and terrifying. He had a girlfriend, a cocktail waitress at a nightclub. Her name was Adele. One night Jack had to go meet some business associates and he left Adele and me at his place. We were drinking heavily. At some point Adele said that she'd recently read something of mine in a magazine and that she really found the style exhilarating and she asked me if I'd take off my clothes so she could see my body. I said OK. Just then Jack came home. He was drunk. He went for me with his knife. I swiveled around and did a modified mambo step and kicked the knife out of his hand and then did a polka backfist and knocked him cold. Adele screamed, pointing to my chest. Jack had slashed me over my right nipple on his first lunge. That's the scar story.'

"She walked me out to the carport.

"Her glazed breasts shimmered in the moonlight.

"Someone had spray-painted 'Death to America!' on my car.

"Not a pretty sight—especially considering the fact that it was a brand-new 1997 Ferrari Testarossa Spider with less than 100 miles on the odometer—not a pretty sight at all . . . but then, coronary arteries clogged with atherosclerotic plaque aren't a very pretty sight either. And that's where Becker Surgical Devices comes in. Becker Surgical Devices, makers of fine percutaneous transluminal coronary angioplasty catheter tubes and balloons, is the overwhelming choice of cardiologists across the country. And remember, Becker Surgical Devices is the official balloon angioplasty instrument supplier for Team Leyner."

"Cut! That was perfect, Mr. Leyner! Absolutely perfect!"

CHAPTER FIVE

INTRODUCTION

In order to rescue my book from the ineluctable current of its own narrative, and in order to resuscitate myself (depressed by an impending divorce, "stupefied in an inner marsh of ennui"), I have decided to work in miniature. Accordingly, Chapter Five shall be comprised of 24 concise segments with headings, in abecedarian sequence.

May God help me. I almost gunned down my father and my elderly grandmother in an expensive nouvelle cuisine restaurant in Boca Raton, Florida, last week. Incensed by the paucity of my $15 appetizer, which consisted of three gossamer-thin shavings of raw filet mignon on a single frond of arugula, and by my grandmother's remark that my pants were inappropriately "heavy" for the summer, and my father's comment that the mole over my right eyebrow had become a "disfigurement," I threw my napkin down on the table and stormed off to the men's room. There, a molten rage seethed within me. I inadvertently reached behind the toilet tank and found, to my utter surprise, a gun taped to the wall. Who had taped the semiautomatic 9-mm pistol to the wall behind the toilet and for what purpose, I had no idea. But I removed the weapon, concealed it under my jacket (à la Napoleon, but with a larger and more conspicuous bulge), and I staggered back toward our table, lurching, careening from side to side, fury playing havoc with my equilibrium. Reaching the table, I withdrew my hand, leveled the weapon at my father, and was about to fire, when I remembered my own preprandial admonition to the thin-lipped, 60-year-old attorney from Jersey City: "Dad, this is our last night with Grandma. She's recovering from cataract surgery. Please don't squabble. Let's make this a special dinner for her." I laid the gun on the table. The restaurant had become deathly quiet. The only sound came from the cappuccino machine, which gurgled intermittently like life-support apparatus in a coma ward. "Short, individually titled sections . . . arranged alphabetically," I murmured dazedly. The maitre d', a heavyset man, cultivated in vitro from embryonic cell buds on a planet within the globular cluster Omega Centauri, wearing a sequined dress inset with points d'esprit, and suffering from spasmodic torticollis—painful neck-muscle spasms that twist the head to one side—would later tell me that the expression on my face was beatific—radiant, yet preternaturally serene. "Like the Little Prince, señor."

That night as I slept in my bed, someone or something apparently drilled an evenly spaced series of tiny holes in my forehead. I hadn't felt anything or even woken up, and only discovered the holes as I stood in front of the bathroom mirror where I begin each morning, monitoring those inevitable daily manifestations of decay—the brown age spots, the broken blood vessels, the wrinkles; some days more appalling matutinal discoveries: maggots, for instance, and once a large piece of pinkish-white brain tissue extruding from one ear—the equivalent of a cerebral hemmorrhoid. Typically these rather sensational "A.M. surprises" subside by the time I have to meet friends or editors or critics for dinner. Even the cerebral hemmorrhoid shrunk back into my head that same day by about 7 P.M. and I was able to join two very powerful Japanese publishing executives at La Côte Basque without embarrassment. But these holes in my forehead were extra-corporeal in origin and, as such, more disturbing. I called Dr. Nils Wachtel. Wachtel was one of the White House "Dr. Feelgoods" who pumped JFK full of speed every day. (Personally—and I think Anna Quindlen might disagree with me on this one—I believe that Congress should make it mandatory that the President of the United States be kept on a continuous amphetamine drip IV. The Commander-in-Chief should be wide awake, 24 hours a day. I don't want a President who wakes up with green gook in his eyes, all groggy, and who's like "What day is it?" [According to an article by military veteran Xiao Ziming in the overseas edition of *The People's Daily* (*Renmin Ribao*), Mao slept only 25 minutes a day—devoting the rest of his time to statecraft, poetry, food, and to pleasuring himself in a specially made vulval-necked Ming vase designed to collect his seed for cryonic preservation. Today the Great Helmsman's sperm is reportedly in the custody of Shining Path guerillas who move the specimens among several secret locations in the Andes via mobile refrigerators strapped to the backs of blindfolded llamas.]

Later at Wachtel's office: "Whoever or whatever did this to you has either an incredibly hard, long, and thin drilling proboscis or used a very sophisticated drill with an advanced-ceramic bit, because these are very tiny but cleanly and precisely drilled holes that go deep into your skull . . . it could even have been some kind of laser.

"Look," he said, after further examination, "there's nothing I can do except patch up the holes with Plastic Skin, which is a kind of dermal spackling. You don't seem to have suffered any kind of neurological damage, so I wouldn't worry."

He suggested that I wear bifocals whose bottom halves were microscopy lenses, enabling me to keep an eye out for any untoward devices or creatures that might appear in my bedroom. But I've found this intolerable because when I use them I become aware of how everything—silverware, drinking glasses, telephone receivers, toothbrushes, even the manuscript pages of the text you are presently enjoying—is covered with a thick layer of dust mite feces.

And as I compose the penultimate paragraph of this Intro, my girlfriend, who's wearing the same iridescent chiffon cocktail dress that she's had on for three days, is lying on the couch, headphones blasting Black Sabbath, guzzling Bacardi 151 until she passes out. Her muzzled rottweiler, sought by the FBI and Interpol in connection with the brutal 1998 mauling of Condor Tisch, Postmaster General under President Hallux Valgus, dreams at her side, its paws twitching spasmodically. Holographic images of celebrities (e.g., Newt Gingrich, Axl Rose), mistakenly transmitted into my home, bang against the closed windows like trapped flies oriented toward the transparency of glass but ignorant of its materiality.

And the tranquillity of the summer evening is shattered by another ten-minute nonstop barrage of projectile vomiting from the fifth-floor suite of the opulent Casa Grundy . . . followed, again, by the ominous whine of a power saw.

AAH!

He's just arrived, apparently having come straight from the gym. The iconic proliferation of his face and body in magazines and newspapers and posters across the country has ironically inured us to the real majesty of his physical presence. Only when confronted by him in person, his face flushed, his hair slicked back, his torso veiny, topographical with muscle, visibly hot from the tremendous workout that professional bodybuilders have called kamikaze-like in its intensity, do we apprehend—with a spine-tingling frisson that I can only compare to my experience as an adolescent of seeing a huge lathery stallion and then a dirigible in rapid succession—how gorgeous he really is. It's almost impossible to conceive that this is the body of an acclaimed writer. And not just an acclaimed writer, but perhaps the most influential writer at work today, certainly the writer who single-handedly brought a generation of young people flocking back to the bookstores after they had purportedly abandoned literature for good. Between mouthfuls of fennel-flavored monkfish, he chats amiably with a group of admirers who've surrounded him. His Ecuadorian girlfriend, wearing a lavender bustier and short chiffon skirt, gazes at him lovingly . . .

—Martha Stewart

It came as something of a surprise to discover that Martha Stewart's August 3rd birthday/housewarming party in East Hampton was merely a pretense to meet me—and not simply to meet me, but to gather material for her adoring profile entitled "Totally Brilliant . . . Totally Buff" which appeared in the September issue of Condé Nast's *Traveler,* and from which the foregoing is excerpted. After all, I'm a ruthless, corrupt, self-indulgent hypocrite; an opportunist, compulsive womanizer, liar, bully, and amphetamine addict. I approach fiction as a great ravenous lion might approach a helpless effete antelope who's lying in the grass stupidly licking the gelatin that oozes from her hooves. Yet sometimes fiction is such docile prey to my depredations that it sickens me, and I feel like abandoning it to the hyenas and focusing my creative powers exclusively on poetry.

I composed a very beautiful poem earlier this morning when I was in my garden, weed-whacking:

> Why did best-selling author Martin Cruz Smith
> testify before a secret Senate subcommittee
> that superlawyer Alan Dershowitz has
> continuously lactating breasts that could someday
> produce up to 50 gallons of milk a day in space?
> Legendary legal eagle F. Lee Bailey and
> sf virtuoso Ray Bradbury debate the issue
> that's tearing the American legal and dairy communities apart.
> Martha Stewart,
> you awaken in me a new fury,
> a new desperation to stun my enemies!
> No family but fans!
> I a hunk, a psycho!

It is rare that a poem so fully realized and of such complexity would arise spontaneously and intact, leaving me to merely rush to my laptop, the loam from my garden darkening the keyboard as I furiously type, verses beginning to fade from memory much as a dream dissipates upon awakening. Aah, if only one could apply a kind of oneiric fixative to dreams before they vanish . . .

C'EST SI BON

In a garden of video sculptures, sleek geometries, Mylar surfaces, and falling water, G. takes off her sweat-soaked tennis shirt—her nipples are covered with two banana daiquiri transdermal patches that transmit the cocktail through her skin into her capillaries—and she breaks off a shard of brittle matzoh and scratches a name on her arm: *Jose Canseco*. He appears, guitar in hand. She hears the faint echo of her doctor's voice, "G., don't give up, fight, please, G., stay with us." It seems so ridiculous, now that G. knows what really happens after you die, now that G. knows how wonderful it really is. Raising her outstretched palm, she urges Canseco to increase the volume of his song. His music is primal and throbbing, his lyrics speak of the open road, of sin, of guns, of steroids, of Madonna. The masturbating zebras, their long slender penises like black and white barber poles, join in on the chorus, the gist of which is simply: "The government is suppressing information about how sweet life after death is."

Of course they are. Why did every single scientist who was working on the secret Life After Death Project commit suicide? Once they found out how fantastic it is, once they realized how shitty life before death is compared to life after death, they raced home to their pistols, pills, razor blades, plastic bags, and exhaust-filled garages. Some were too impatient to even endure the commute home and—too eager to even wait for the elevator—they raced 30 stories up the stairwell to the roof of the institute and leapt with the exultant whoops of children pouring from the schoolyard in the last days of June.

DIAMOND HEAD

She was Rachel, the Lubavitcher girl. Rachel lived a pious studious life, studying the Torah. She'd never ventured much beyond the confines of the Crown Heights section of Brooklyn. But one night she and two of her girlfriends went to Chinatown. And there she met Nguyen Du, a member of Born to Kill, the craziest, most violent Vietnamese gang in New York. So began the love story that would turn two families, two communities, two cultures inside out. Only Mark Leyner—who underwent cosmetic surgery (blepharoplasty) and lived with Born to Kill for a year, eating, sleeping, and stealing with them, frequenting their haunts (Maria's coffee shop on Lafayette Street and the Tung Nam Har mall on Canal)—could capture the pathos, the humor, and the garish violence of this incendiary romance. Imagine Chaim Potok collaborating with Amy Tan and Iceberg Slim. Imagine *Fiddler on the Roof* starring Bruce Lee. Imagine *Miss Saigon* with book by Martin Buber and music by Booger Storm, a garage "cai luong" band from suburban Da Nang. Your heart will melt when Rachel's eyes meet Nguyen's for the very first time. You'll squirm in your reading chair during the extraordinary mystical battle scenes between Rachel's Kabbalah-wielding father and Nguyen's cousin, an I Ching–toting Taoist alchemist. You'll weep big-time when Born to Kill assassins machine-gun the synagogue during Nguyen's bar mitzvah. You'll become dizzy, perhaps even nauseous, as you're catapulted from the kosher pizzerias of midtown Manhattan's diamond district to the chaotic fish markets of Mott Street. But love conquers all in this vertiginous bildungsroman of the human heart. In an unforgettable tour de force of impressionistic reportage, Leyner follows Rachel and Nguyen on their honeymoon to a bed and breakfast inn near the malfunctioning Platte River nuclear power plant. Nguyen visits the sarcophagus-like reactor and absorbs massive amounts of gamma radiation, which inexplicably enables him to travel through time. You'll gnash your teeth and tear the hair from your head when Rachel decides that she has no other choice but to accept Nguyen's decision to travel back in history and attempt to have sex with civilization's most luminary women, women whom Nguyen has secretly lusted after ever since his junior high school history class. You'll teeter on the edge of your seat as Nguyen, working against a tightly scheduled itinerary, tries to score with the likes of Joan of Arc, Queen Victoria, Madame Curie, Florence Nightingale, Edith Piaf, Babe Didrikson, and Amelia Earhart. Meanwhile, inexplicably, Rachel has been sent to live on a commune populated by a terrifying assortment of psychopaths: serial killers, neo-Nazi skinheads, cocaine-cartel hitmen, "angel of death" hospital orderlies, etc. Imagine Nathaniel Hawthorne's utopian, socialistic community in his novel *The Blithedale Romance*—but now imagine it inhabited by Ed Gein, Richard Speck, Charles Manson, John Wayne Gacy, Son of Sam, Mark David Chapman, Ted Bundy, Jeffrey Dahmer, etc. Rachel's escape from this egalitarian pit of evil (engineered by an intrepid team of Hasidic Ninjas, masters of night stealth in their black fedoras and frock coats) and her ultimate reunion with Nguyen comprise one of the most electrifying narrative sequences in modern literature. But all is not quite peaches and cream (or perhaps we should say, kreplach and nuoc mam). Rachel is anguished by what she perceives as Nguyen's abandonment of her. Although Nguyen has converted to Judaism, learned Yiddish, and forsworn the drug peddling and gunplay that characterized his youth, Rachel feels that she will never again trust him sufficiently for an intimate relationship. Enter Dr. Harriet Raeburn, couples therapist extraordinaire. Remember Sybil's therapist—the one who patiently integrated Sally Field's swarm of personalities? Remember Dr. Martin T. Orne, poet Anne Sexton's psychiatrist who first persuaded Anne to write down her feelings and add line breaks? Harriet Raeburn is such a therapist. You'll cry tears of joy when after only nine years of weekly couple therapy, Rachel and Nguyen are able to again communicate without physical violence and are able to look into each other's eyes with the longing and passion of that first night at the New Viet Huong on Mulberry Street.

Un-fucking-believable, right? What would you think if I told you that I conceived of that entire scenario—word for word—in about two minutes, between sets of incline bench presses? I still have to figure out how to incorporate Camp Schreckensherrschaft, a weight-loss camp for terrorists that I found advertised in the back pages of *The Sunday Times Magazine*. The camp's run by a guy called the Schreckenmeister (the Terror Master), an erstwhile operative for the notorious East German security service Stasi, who'd reputedly been cashiered because of a weight problem, and who then dedicated himself to training obese terrorists to lose weight and keep it off. A list of this guy's clients reads like a who's who of international terrorism: Carlos the Jackal (who was once known as Carlos the Hippo), Ulrike Meinhof, Abu Nidal, Abimael Guzman (the founder of Peru's Sendero Luminoso), plus scores of formerly overweight members of the Japanese Red Army, the IRA, the ETA (the Basque-autonomist underground organization), plus many more! You'll be shocked and amazed by the story of how the Schreckenmeister helped Renato Curcio—the Red Brigade mastermind of the Aldo Moro kidnapping—lose over 75 pounds simply by replacing whole milk ricotta and mozzarella cheese with low- or no-fat substitutes in his favorite dishes!

Here's the chilling account of my first meeting with the "Terror Master":

> It was beautiful the way the sunlight filtered through the louvered blinds casting vertical slats of thermal illumination on the section of his face left intact. Most of the face was gone, mangled and riven on the battlefield or in the torture chambers of his enemies. There was a jagged swath of forehead, a bubbled crimson knob of cheekbone, and an eye, merciless and abstracted—these the last remaining vestiges of natal physiognomy; the rest was prosthetic—a filtrated perforation in lieu of nostrils, servomechanical jaws with ceramic-fiber-reinforced metal teeth, and polyurethane tongue. I stood there transfixed, as if before a masterpiece in a museum.
> "I'm Mark Leyner," I finally managed to mumble.
> He extended his hand, tautly sheathed in a blue latex glove.
> "I am the Schreckenmeister."

Pretty chilling, huh? I also have to figure out how to incorporate the former NBA player who's been programmed to kill whenever he hears Stevie Wonder's "I Just Called to Say I Love You" played at the wrong speed.

And I have to figure out how to incorporate the quartet of fifties-style a cappella vocalists who were performing for bauxite miners in Ghana when there was an explosion and cave-in, trapping the satin-suited lounge act almost two miles underground.

Here's the stirring account of their rescue:

> The singers are alive! The excavation team—grimy, exhausted, yet ever determined—is raising its blistered hands in joyous unison. The foreman puts his stethoscope to the ground and bids the crew, media representatives, and assembled onlookers to quiet down. He's listening . . . he's smiling . . . he's beginning to snap his fingers. "They're alive all right!" he's saying, apparently discerning a very faint but unmistakable "doo wop doo wop . . . doo wop doo wop."

Pretty stirring, huh?

FEELINGS

Today my marble citadel looms high above the asphalt, which is littered with the sun-bleached skeletons of my enemies. My dog Carmella wears a gold Rolex just above each of her four paws. I'm often seen dining at Spago, L.A.'s enduringly glamour-packed eatery, or strutting around Yemen in a full-length ermine coat, a hooker on each arm. Just yesterday, I was invited by ABC's "The American Sportsman" to go to Australia to hunt bandicoots with aboriginal boomerangs along with Ken Follett and Whitley Strieber. Bergdorf's is charging $3,500 for a hand-carved Baccarat crystal bottle of "Team Leyner," the perfume. (Forty million scent strips have been inserted in October and November issues of *Vogue, Harper's Bazaar, Elle, Vanity Fair, Mirabella, Glamour,* and *Mademoiselle.*)

What's a typical day like for Mark Leyner?
   Yesterday, after a long afternoon of volunteer bereavement counseling and then reading to blind residents at a local nursing home, I go to Le Cirque. I drink something like 14 martinis. I get into a fight at the bar with the president of the Jersey City firefighters' union over a woman we're both trying to pick up. I kill him with a single roundhouse kick to the side of his head. I

leave with the woman, who's cooing to me in a gravelly basso profundo voice. When we get to my apartment, I dump out the contents of her pocketbook: loaded jade-handled pistol, Quaaludes, Thai "golden eggs" (vibrating anal-stimulation balls), a packet of pharmaceutical-grade morphine, a little black book with the private phone numbers of Pentagon officials. I get up on the bed and dance to the electronic music they use to drive fleas and cockroaches crazy, my hard-on glowing in the dark and keeping time like a metronome, and then we fuck until dawn, strangling each other almost to the point of unconsciousness with kimono sashes each time we climax.

The next morning, I prepare a Jerusalem artichoke and spinach salad, stewed rabbit in white wine, and a pureed chestnut and chocolate layer cake, and I bring it over to Sister Norberta for the homeless shelter she runs at the church. I write for the rest of the day—extended, lyrical, almost psalm-like meditations on the redemptiveness of love.

Will I ever reconcile my inner contradictions? Is it so terribly wrong to live the way I do?

GAMMA GLOBULIN, UP, OLIVES

Many of the great American poets of the late 20th century murdered Hollywood stars (perhaps to silence their shrill insipidity), but what were their writing habits?

The man who killed Kevin Costner, flayed him, and wore his skin eschewed the computer keyboard; he preferred to write his poetry in longhand, producing an indecipherable rebus of printed letters, script, numerical formulae, and pictures.

But Jesus! What a strange rich beautiful music was frozen in the inscrutability of these hieroglyphs, waiting to be awakened by the warm kiss of an expert's exegesis, like cryonically preserved Vedic birds, thawed, and tweeting recondite ragas!

After a day of painful labor (he was a rigorous, fanatically self-critical, self-flagellating slave to his muse, and his progress from line to line and stanza to stanza was torturously slow), he would drive to town and stand in the middle of 7 Eleven, garbed in Costner's flesh from head to toe—in a unitard of Costner's skin—and he would affect Costner's bovine gaze and Costner's uninflected speech pattern, and recite those weirdly buoyant and long long lyrics to hapless customers, many immobile with horror, some amused and snickering.

How profoundly sad that he considered these often chemically dependent nocturnal nomads his public!

How profoundly sad that during his lifetime only isolated and ineffectual academics would apprehend the preternatural vivacity and divine fabric of his mind.

And the woman who smothered Julia Roberts—she is perhaps my favorite fin de siècle poet of all!

In "The Florist of Agony," in measured stanzas simultaneously candid and marmoreal, she tells the story of two anthropologists—one very smart and domineering and one very stupid and obsequious—who travel to a part of Amazonia heretofore "unmolested by civilization." They encounter a tribe of fierce, headshrinking, hallucinogen-snorting people who befriend them and allow them to live in their village as kin. But soon, through a series of comically abortive sexual encounters with pubescent girls, the tall, sleazy anthropologist discovers that the tribespeople are robots. Who built them? No one knows. Perhaps a tribe of sophisticated rain forest inhabitants who lived thousands of years ago and committed mass suicide rather than face a time when people like Costner, Roberts, Alec Baldwin, Demi Moore, Kiefer Sutherland, Charlie Sheen, and Emilio Estevez would be considered "stars." Or perhaps they were cannibalized by their own robotic progeny—severely tonsured, squat, broad-nosed "Indians," the women naked save for feather appurtenances, the men wearing only penis strings.

MAILBAG

Dear Mark,

First of all, I'd just like to say what tremendous pleasure your books have given my entire family. My wife and I just think that you're an out-and-out American genius of the highest magnitude. The kids think that reading your fiction is "excellent—like being on drugs," and they both want to be writers, thanks to you. We all loved Martha Stewart's piece on you in *Traveler*—please say "buenos dias" to your Ecuadorian girlfriend for us! We've recently read articles in the *Enquirer* and the *Star* about how distracting your divorce from Arleen has been for you and how it might significantly delay the completion of your new book and we've heard rumors about your violent mood swings from steroids and about how they and the Lincoln's morning breath scandal may have cost you lucrative endorsement contracts for Ore-Ida Tater Tots and, more importantly, for Phallotropin—the new synthetic Penile Growth Hormone from Genitotech, and about how the government's punitive confiscation program is eating away at your net worth, and how Team Leyner has become a miasma of antagonism, misunderstanding, and mutual suspicion, and about how there's sectarian strife within the elderly bionic security force, and about how Baby Lago defected and went to work for Tom Clancy, and we'd just like to say that we don't believe any of it, and we look forward to your new book with great excitement and anticipation.

Ed Audet
Cicero, NY

115

Dear [insert name],

Thanks so much for your kind words. Although my busy schedule does not permit me to personally respond to the tremendous volume of adulatory mail that I receive, I'd like to send you and your family an official Team Leyner gift. Please indicate on the enclosed business reply card which exciting premium you'd like rushed to your home.

A. One slow-release polymer matrix system *LeynerHead Sublingual Software Lozenge* that, placed under the tongue, provides you with the sensation of being a sinewy and licentious pop icon (do not use LeynerHead software lozenge if you have a hernia or difficulty in urination due to enlargement of prostate gland).

B. *Finley PantryMaid*—Performance artist Karen Finley, who provoked the wrath of conservatives across the country when she received federal grants for performances that included shoving yams up her ass, has now angered many of her supporters by signing a multimillion-dollar licensing deal with the Pantry-Maid Company. PantryMaid will be making a plastic "Karen Finley Kitchen Canister." The container, molded into a scale model of Finley's ass with a screw-top anus, will allow you to store not only yams, but rice, candy, leftover beef Bourguignon . . . whatever you want. Here's a microwavable, dishwasher-safe kitchen container with a dash of downtown-intellectual cachet. Team Leyner is proud to offer you—as an absolutely free gift premium—the Finley PantryMaid, which is not yet available in any store!

C. *Ahfongool!: Petrarchan Love Sonnets by John Gotti*—Experience a facet of the "Dapper Don" that you don't often read about in the tabloids. This collection of ardent, elegantly crafted Petrarchan love sonnets, composed by the *capo di tutti capi* of the Gambino crime family between 1983 and 1992, is masterfully translated from the Italian by the esteemed Richard Howard, winner of a National Book Award for his rendering from Yiddish to English of Meyer Lansky's Talmudic commentaries. This exquisite first-edition book, with Italian and English lyrics printed on facing pages, bound in leather with richly hubbed spines ornamented in 22-karat gold and produced with gilded page edges and specially milled acid-free paper, will be a treasured addition to your heirloom library. *Ahfongool!* is a "must-have" for bibliophiles everywhere!

D. *The Complete Guide to Forensic Musicology*—a comprehensive sourcebook exploring this fascinating and revolutionary field in which scientists, by studying molecular changes in the ear's cochlea, can determine what music homicide or suicide victims were listening to at the time of their deaths.

Dear Mark,

My girlfriend and I have a bet over who's older, soul crooner Isaac Hayes or Dash Crofts of Seals & Crofts. I say Hayes. (Whoever wins has to be the other one's sex slave for 24 hours.)

Lewis Pavlik
Boonton, NJ

Dear Lewis,

I hope you sprinkled a lot of Spanish fly on your Wheaties this morning. Isaac Hayes was born on August 20, 1942, making him 49 years old. Crofts performed his first extrauterine concert on August 14, 1940, putting 51 candles on his B'day Twinkie. Enjoy your captivity while it lasts, big guy.

Dear Mark,

You're playing tennis with your father. It's a brutally hot and humid afternoon. The other courts are empty, apparently no one else is willing to play in this stifling heat. You and your father have each won a set apiece. The score of the third and deciding set is six games to five, you're serving at 40–30, match point. Your father's face is flushed, his breathing is labored. You hit a 112-miles-an-hour serve wide to his backhand. He grunts as he lurches toward the sideline, barely getting his racket on the ball, but managing to return it. He groans, apparently having severely twisted—perhaps even sprained or broken—his ankle. Sensing a diminution of his mobility, you float a delicate drop shot just over the net with so much backspin that it barely rises from the ground. Your father limps desperately in from backcourt, clutching his chest with one hand, and he lunges toward the ball, tumbling to the hot asphalt surface, scraping sections of flesh off his knees and elbows, but amazingly getting the ball back over the net, but not deep into your court. You decide to take advantage of his obvious fatigue and battered legs. You lob over his head, forcing him to backpedal as fast as he can in order to save the point, the set, and the match. In the still sultry air, you can hear him wheeze as he struggles back, back, back . . . and flicks his racket head at the ball, managing an absolutely last-ditch survival-lob that sends the ball back high into the shallow court—a perfect setup for your game-, set-, and match-winning overhead smash. As you keep your eyes focused on the ball and you bend your knees and arch your back in preparation for the authoritative winner, you notice, out of the corner of your eye, that your father has collapsed. Do you forgo the winning smash, leap over the net, and rush to your father's assistance? Or do you hit the overhead, winning the hard-fought match, and then rush to your father's aid? Mr. Leyner, you make the call.

Greg Hayes
Evansville, IN

Dear Greg,

Nietzsche wrote: "What is good?—All that enhances the feeling of power, the Will to Power, and power itself in man. What is bad?—All that proceeds from weakness. What is happiness?—The feeling that power is increasing."

Hit the smash, win the match, and then rush to your stricken father's aid. Your father, from the symptoms you've described—flushed face, labored breathing, severe chest pains—has apparently suffered a massive coronary. It's doubtful that the time it takes to win the point will cost your father much in terms of his survivability. Don't let the last thing your father sees you do be an act of abject sentiment and weakness. Execute the overhead with joyful ferocity. You win, your father loses. Victory is good. Be happy.

SQUIRMELIA

Squirmelia, miniature and dark (a.k.a. "Yuca D."; a.k.a. "Kid Woman"), retreats to her aluminum tanning shack near Casino Lens Loch to eat Double Shells, bivalve pasta shapes in a creamy lime sauce.

Her estranged boyfriend has been on a submarine for four years.

Off in a funnel of distance, where the quantum infrastructure of the lake is turned inside out (i.e., on the anti-lake), the desultory dance of the reddish-purple prolapsed rectums of the aged busboys can be seen as the stooped septuagenarians dismantle the table umbrellas on the crepe-swathed deck of the steamboat, al fresco dining deemed high-risk due to an impending downpour of asteroid shrapnel.

Squirmelia eats, grinning methodically, wondering how she will explain to Vinnie all that's changed since he joined the Sikh navy. Like how Rei Kawakubo was invited to design the uniforms of the suicide squad of dental hygienists who floss the comatose sea monster's teeth, and how she refused.

I can't seem to vaporize Squirmelia's brains by staring into her eyes ardently.

In my hammock, I listen to the rain hit my helmet and wonder if it's true or simply my mother's fanciful apocrypha that as a child I'd listen to the patter of space stones on the aluminum roof of the "museum" where Father kept my brain-dead brother alive, impaled with hundreds of fish hooks, and I'd discern winning Lotto numbers.

Like ballistic war-cannoli that fly through the sky and plunge into people's mouths at incredible speeds, rigid microscopic larval creatures hurtle through time.

THREE HUNDRED
MILLIGRAMS OF
DIANOBOL

"**I** drink it black."

"You're the best lover I ever had. Last night . . . the pleasure you gave me was so fucking unbelievably intense . . . I felt like I was going to disintegrate cell by cell. Eggs?"

"A dozen egg whites scrambled, baby. Kippers. Rye toast. Can I help with anything?"

"Well, uh . . . there's this real creep who moved in next door and . . . he's sort of been . . . well, bothering me."

"What do you mean, bothering you?"

"Well, grabbing at me in the hallway, saying disgusting perverted things to me under his breath . . ."

"Call an ambulance."

"An ambulance? Are you OK?"

"I'm fine. And I'll be right back. Tell them to get here as quickly as possible."

I was dressed in casual but expensive clothes. I stripped down to my bikini briefs and went next door.

I was back in five minutes.

"What happened? I heard three thuds."

"Two thuds were me breaking his hands. One thud was me breaking his jaw. So he won't be grabbing at you anymore and he won't be saying disgusting perverted things to you. Are you OK? You're trembling and panting."

"I'm so turned on by you. Can I smell you?"

"Yes."

She pressed her face to my chest and inhaled.

"You smell so good . . . it's like cloves . . . mushrooms . . . caramel . . . vanilla . . . popcorn . . . roast potatoes . . . cooked apples . . . fried fat. I'm so glad that my sister-in-law introduced me to you!" she said.

"Ditto," I replied laconically.

"Also, Mark, I just wanted to tell you that I think it's so amazing that you won the competition to design the new Museum of Contemporary Art. You were competing against some real heavyweights—I. M. Pei, Frank Gehry, Robert Venturi, Michael Graves, Peter Eisenman—and you won without ever having taken a single architecture course, without, in fact, ever having made a single architectural sketch before!"

"I'm outa here."

"OK, Mark. Will I see you again?"

"Uh . . . maybe I'll . . . uh . . . I don't know if . . . uh . . ."

"Mark, what's the matter?"

"I don't know if the problem is that I'm incapable of expressing myself adequately or if my feelings are too inchoate, too amorphous, perhaps too puerile to even warrant expression."

"I love you."

"Call me sometime. That's as much of a commitment as I can make right now."

I wrote my first play quite late in life. In fact, it wasn't until I was almost 25 years old that I entered a theater for the first time. I carried a metal pail of candy corn in one hand and a pail of soda in the other—I was straight from the countryside, a strapping libidinal bumpkin, utterly unsophisticated. (I'd gone to see Ida

Villanueva in *Green Wind, Black Kites,* a film about a man who spends four days at a Robert Bly "Wild Man" workshop at which every dish is made out of garbanzo beans—e.g., faux steak tartare and faux blood sausage, both meatless and consisting solely of garbanzo beans and clever seasoning—and when he returns home he locks himself in a closed unventilated garage and asphyxiates himself on his own intestinal gas. The movie hinges on the question of whether he should be considered a suicide—thereby making his wife ineligible to collect his death benefits—or whether he should be considered a moron who has accidentally rid future generations of his genetic toxicity in the self-cleaning oven of Darwinian evolution, in which case his wife should be rewarded under the insurance company's innovative "green" eco-bonus policy—double indemnity for the spouses of policyholders who die making a contribution to the health of the planet. Angie Dickinson plays the grieving widow, Gene Hackman plays the gutsy insurance adjuster who lobbies for her eco-bonus, falls deeply in love with her, and is eventually pecked to death by a 175-pound genetically engineered gamecock, while trying to disrupt a cockfight sanctioned by the Venezuelan Institute of Biotechnology in Caracas. Ida Villanueva plays a beautiful and temperamental violin prodigy, longing to be loved, but distrustful of the men she so gladly exploits, who, by film's end, has degenerated into a frumpy, vulgar, and castrating middle-aged shrew.)

And so you see, "the theater" as a cultural institution, certainly as an expressive prerogative, did not even enter my consciousness until I was an adult. While ambitious young tyros were honing their playwriting skills in MFA programs, poring over their Marlowe, their Ibsen and O'Neill, I was ensconced in my basement "laboratory," manipulating the size of my scrotum with a recombinant strain of filarial elephantiasis that I'd developed. (Filarial elephantiasis, in its natural form, leaves its victims with grotesquely deformed limbs and sometimes with scrota the size of basketballs. But precise titration of my altered strain allowed me to capriciously enlarge or shrink my scrotum with impunity.)

At that stage of my life, walking through a shopping mall with a pair of gigantic testicles ballooning the crotch of my jeans was an infinitely more compelling pastime than sitting in a library carrel, scribbling marginalia in a copy of *Mourning Becomes Electra*.

And, in all candor, it still is.

VARICOSE MOON

A Play in One Act

CHARACTERS:
The Prerecorded Voice
The Host
The Contestant
The Audience

SETTING: A television studio in Pyongyang, North Korea

THE PRERECORDED VOICE: Slight in stature, but volcanic in temperament, I became dedicated in 1969 to transforming myself into, first, a sullen, violent, willfully inarticulate teenage boy who was enthralling to ebullient, chatty, earnest teenage girls; and then to evolving into a truly explosive, erotic, fetishistic corporeal object, lean and muscled like an ex-con cowboy. I include myself in this developmental category along with Lenny Dykstra, Napoleon Bonaparte, and others.

So can I be enthralling to women today by obsessively projecting a cartoon version of my adolescent fantasy-self? So far the answer is "Yes! We want more!" Is this somehow related to heavy-metal? Yes, probably. Did Melville, Flaubert, Conrad, Austen, et al psych themselves up to face the empty page by staring at their bare torsos in the mirror or by sinking even deeper into the narcissistic contemplation of an even smaller frame of that image, e.g., the silver skull nestled in the hairy cleavage of a pumped chest? The answer must be no. But then I don't think that those folks wrote to enhance their fuckability.

My books and my body—my status as a reckless writer and a gorgeous man—are my iridescent plumage; they're the equivalent of the male *L. ocellatus* frog's 250- to 500-hertz call made to maintain territoriality and to attract mates; they're the equivalent of the peculiar ritual of the male pyrochroidae beetle displaying to a potential mate a deep cleft in his forehead. Stashed within the cleft is a small dose of the chemical cantharidin; during courtship, the male exposes his cleft to the female, she grabs his head and immediately laps up the chemical offering. Apparently placated, she allows the male to mate. Scientists have determined that the male transfers to the female a much larger quantity of cantharidin during intercourse, and that she subsequently incorporates the chemical into her eggs, which thenceforth are protected against ants and other common predators of beetle eggs.

My books and my body: my not-so-subliminal advertisement to women that I will make a primo contribution to the genetic makeup and survivability of their children.

It's the night. I spread my cerebral hemispheres and display my chemical offering. Who will grab my head and immediately lap it up?

THE CONTESTANT (rising from his seat in the audience): I will! I'll grab your head and immediately lap up your chemical offering!

THE HOST: Well, come on down!!

[**THE CONTESTANT** runs wildly down the aisle, waving his arms, and mounts the stage.]

THE HOST: It's great to have you on the show!

THE CONTESTANT: It's great to be here! I love the show! I made this for you!

THE HOST: That's fantastic! It's a beautiful ring . . . what is this here, amber?

THE CONTESTANT: It's a forty-million-year-old chunk of amber in which a female fungus gnat was embedded, Bob.

THE HOST: Incredible! It says here you're married.

THE CONTESTANT: I'm married, Bob, and I have a beautiful mistress who just turned twenty. And my wife is a boozer and she has a lover.

THE HOST: It says here that your wife's lover doesn't use spoken language to communicate, that he communicates with a complex vocabulary of exuded chemicals.

THE CONTESTANT: That's right, Bob, my wife uses a gas chromatograph and ion-trap mass spectrometer to analyze the chemical content of his "message secretions" and then a computer to translate the chemical sequences into English.

THE HOST: Where did your wife meet this fascinating lover?

THE CONTESTANT: In the yard, Bob.

THE HOST: And where did you meet your mistress?

THE CONTESTANT: At The Gap, Bob.

THE HOST: It says here that you're the president of the Brine Shrimp Council.

THE CONTESTANT: That's right, Bob. We live in an increasingly complex and technological society, and we find that for real, honest, old-fashioned food enjoyment, more and more people are turning to delicious, half-inch-long brine shrimp raised in space.

THE HOST: In space?

THE CONTESTANT: Yes, Bob. They're part of a food chain for astronauts in space stations. Algae feed on the solid waste of the astronauts and in turn are consumed by the brine shrimp, which grow about a half-inch long. Astronauts then eat the brine shrimp. We thought, what the hey, why should astronauts have all the fun? For the first time, we're now making available to the public all-natural astronaut-poop-fed-algae-fed brine shrimp shuttled directly to our plant daily from orbiting space stations. You like shrimp scampi, Bob?

THE HOST: Ummmmmm. I love it.

THE CONTESTANT: Try our mouth-watering, half-inch, space-station-raised brine shrimp prepared scampi-style. It's a taste sensation you'll never forget.

THE HOST: It says here that you have trouble trusting other people.

THE CONTESTANT: That's right, Bob. It's probably related to something that happened to me when I was a kid.

My grandmother, who'd always seemed like a sweet, kind, indulgent old lady, went out for a pack of cigarettes one day. I happened to be at the newspaper stand that afternoon leafing through the latest muscle magazines. Grandma didn't see me right away—I had my back to the register. She asked for a pack of Lucky Strikes and I recognized her voice and I turned around and said, "Nana, hello." She looked insane. She grabbed me and dragged me outside.

"I'm not the Nana I appear to be, kid," she said.

"What do you mean?" I asked, trying to squirm out of her grasp. I'd never realized how physically strong she was or how masculine her body odor was when she exerted herself.

"I've got a Grandma facade, but inside I'm the most un-Grandma-like creature on earth."

" 'Un-Grandma-like' how?" I asked, not ready to accept this challenge to my idealized version of the doting, potato-pancake-making, warm-hearted geriatric.

"What if I told you that I'm a total slut, that I give blow-jobs to all your friends on the football team, that I have a female lover—an ex-Marine who's a bouncer at a bar in Key West—that I attacked a mailman with a baseball bat when I lived in Spain and he's been a brain-damaged vegetable ever since, although he can still get erections . . . and that's how I conceived your father."

"You mean you attacked Grandpa with a baseball bat and then sat on his poor insensate erection to get your own sick jollies and that's how my dad was conceived?"

"That's right. That's your grandfather. You always thought he had a stroke, right?"

I was getting pissed at her now. "You're a liar!"

She spit on the street. "Fuck you, kid. You're just too much of a naive baby to accept the truth."

Just then, these guys jumped out of a van parked across the street. "Surprise!" they yelled.

"What's going on?" I asked.

"Tell him, Grandma," one of them said.

And she said: "Mark, you're on 'America's Favorite Secret Videos!' " (Or "America's Funniest Covert Surveillance Videos" or something—I don't remember the exact name of the show, some rewarmed version of "Candid Camera.")

I was deeply hurt by the whole episode. I felt that my Grandma had betrayed me. But no one in my family understood how I felt.

My parents and my sister were all excited about Grandma and me being on TV and they couldn't understand what my problem was. They had no idea how embarrassed I felt about the video and how mortified I'd be when all my friends saw it. And they had no inkling of how painful and profoundly disillusioning it was to have my own grandmother behave in such a dishonest and treacherous way to me.

THE AUDIENCE: [Applause]

THE HOST: OK, let's get started!

THE CONTESTANT: "Team Leyner" for $100, Bob.

THE HOST: "When he was in the third grade, he had stationery printed up that said 'From the word processor of Mario Puzo . . .' and he'd write these unbelievably prolix, baroque, hallucinatory, torridly erotic mash notes to the female teachers at his elementary school.

"Today, farmers let their land lie fallow after having visions of his semen raining down from the sky and fecundating their fields. Wives refuse to get out of bed, remaining supine, their legs spread in the air, declining to even roll onto their sides lest a drop of his precious fluid leak from their vaginas, after dreaming that he's floated into their bedrooms like a muscle-bound incubus and made love to them, bringing them to seismic, apocalyptic orgasms with one single stroke of his unearthly dick. . . ."

THE CONTESTANT: Who is Mark Leyner?

THE HOST: "Who is Mark Leyner?" is correct, for $100!

THE AUDIENCE: [Applause]

THE CONTESTANT: "Team Leyner" for $500, Bob.

THE HOST: "The worst thing that can happen to a man is to die anonymous. You can be a sensitive guy, really in touch with your feelings, gentle and loving to your wife and kids, active in all sorts of charitable organizations, you can tithe 75 percent of your income to Amnesty International or Habitat for Humanity, etc. etc., but then one day, you die—and outside of your friends and family, who gives a fuck? Nobody. You came, you went, no one remembers, no one cares. It's a tragedy. Because this is the critical difference between a human being and an animal—the capability to be famous. There are exceptions, like Secretariat or Willard or Flipper, but generally, only a human being can make himself immortal with renown. This is your destiny. But die unknown, and you will disgrace me, and I will endlessly grovel through the streets of eternity, eating garbage and mumbling incoherent nonsense."

THE CONTESTANT: What did Mark Leyner's mother whisper as she nuzzled him to her breast immediately after his birth?

THE HOST: That's absolutely right, for $500!

THE AUDIENCE: [Applause]

THE CONTESTANT: "Team Leyner" for $750, Bob.

THE HOST: "The size of a Ping-Pong ball, it's fifty times as large as that of a normal heterosexual male's."

THE CONTESTANT: What is the third interstitial nucleus of Mark Leyner's hypothalamus?

THE HOST: You got it, for $750!

THE AUDIENCE: [Applause]

THE CONTESTANT: "Team Leyner" for $1,000, Bob.

[There's a deafening arpeggio of sirens.]

THE HOST: It's Double or Trouble!

THE AUDIENCE: [Jubilant shouting and stomping]

THE HOST: You can risk your entire winnings to double your money with a correct answer for a total of $4,700 or you can play it safe for the $1,000.

THE CONTESTANT: I'll risk it all! Double or Trouble, Bob!

THE AUDIENCE: [Thunderous ovation]

THE HOST: Her father founded TV-OLFATO, the first global smell-a-vision network, whose inaugural broadcast was "Que Oloroso!" an olfactory portrait of Julio Iglesias, beamed across Central and South America on September 10, 1994. Known variously as "Kid Woman," "Yuka D.," and "Squirmelia," she consummated her affair with Leyner on a "bed" of plastic bubble wrap in a Bloomingdale's stockroom.

THE CONTESTANT: Who is the Ecuadorian girlfriend?

[There's an explosion, then a huge flash and shockwave. Black, acrid smoke fills the studio. When the air finally begins to clear, shattered glass and other debris can be seen littering the ground. The metal grid that supported various lights and microphones is mangled and twisted. THE AUDIENCE is cheering ecstatically.]

THE HOST: That's exactly right! Double or Trouble for $4,700!!

THE AUDIENCE: [More wild cheering]

THE CONTESTANT: Let's stick with "Team Leyner" for $5,000, Bob.

THE HOST: This Team Leyner honcho defected from the organization and wrote a shocking exposé. After hearing the title of his or her book, identify the honcho: *Megalomania's Mascot: My Life with the Team Leyner Cult* (As told to Cleveland Amory).

THE CONTESTANT: Who is Carmella?

THE HOST: "Who is Carmella?" is absolutely correct, for $5,000!

THE AUDIENCE: [Applause]

THE CONTESTANT: "Team Leyner" for $10,000, Bob.

THE HOST: "After their resignations were angrily rejected by a raving, wild-eyed Leyner who'd taken to wearing a lavishly bemedaled military uniform and a booby-trapped truss (apparently to be detonated in case of capture), Desiree Buttcake and the elderly bodyguards were placed in a polyvinylchloride kiddie pool filled with powdered poi mix (a desperate, ruthless Leyner threatening to add water) and surrounded by an 18-foot-high fence topped with concertina wire and electrified with 400 volts and guarded by a rudimentary cyborg pig who'd been jerry-built from spare laboratory cadaver organs and obsolete computer components. (In the final days, Leyner personally constructed the so-called 'hog of vigilance,' naming it 'Mahapuna' after the sow warrior-goddess of Hawaiian mythology.) It featured an old bulky Radio Shack 'brain' with only 32 kilobytes of RAM, its cardiopulmonary system was powered by 17 hamster hearts rigged in tandem, and its prosthetic cloven hooves were made out of plastic vacuum cleaner casters. Although capable of limited ambulation and of digesting small amounts of slop, it was incapable of snorting, rooting for truffles, and other characteristically porcine behaviors, making it the object of constant derision from disgruntled Team Leyner staffers. Using small amounts of cleverly concealed Czechoslovak-made Semtex plastic explosive, Buttcake and the bodyguards managed to escape from Team Leyner Headquarters in the middle of the night. After three weeks of wandering the countryside, during which time they subsisted on hailstones, discarded pizza crusts scavenged from frat house dumpsters, and ultimately, when even this meager food source became unavailable, licking the dried sweat from the earpieces of each other's sunglasses, they sought and were granted asylum in this posh Westchester County community founded by the owner of a popular Italian fast-food franchise."

THE CONTESTANT: What is Sbarro-on-Hudson?

THE HOST: Right you are, for $10,000!

THE AUDIENCE: [Applause]

THE CONTESTANT: Let it ride, Bob. "Team Leyner" for $25,000!

THE AUDIENCE: [Applause]

THE HOST: "Certain muscles were so convex, so protuberant, so cantilevered, that they kept the areas beneath them completely shaded from the sun. So his body was mottled red and white. His torso was cubist. And I'd come home from a grueling ten-hour day of back-to-back sessions with clients, and I'd find this two-tone cubist troglodyte on the floor of his office, completely naked, a tampon string hanging out of his ass, softly ranting into a tape recorder, and I'd think to myself, I just can't take this much longer. Nothing in all my training as a psychotherapist prepared me for marriage with a man so relentless in his effort to construct a self out of the fabric of pure delusion, a man whose valuation of other human beings was so warped that he was, at any instant, capable of terrifying outbursts of cruelty and violence. We went to a computer store one day because Mark needed a new daisy wheel for his printer, and he asked the salesclerk if they sold a daisy wheel with the Tifanagh font. Tifanagh is an obscure medieval script used by Berber women for writing love poetry—of course they didn't carry it, no company even manufactures such a thing. But Mark became absolutely crazed. He grabbed a surge protector off the shelf and beat the clerk quite badly. It's only because the cops who responded to the owner's frantic 911 call were big fans of Mark's books that he wasn't arrested. A similar incident occurred at Sears one morning. We were shopping for gardening supplies and Mark asked a salesperson—a kid who couldn't have been more than sixteen—if Sears sold bags of Raptor Pellets. Raptor pellets are hair-and-bone balls regurgitated by birds of prey. The poor kid gave us this befuddled shrug and Mark went nuts. Mark's got a tremendously powerful throwing arm—he pitched, I believe, four or five no-hitters in a single season when he played semi-pro ball down in the Galápagos Islands. Now, I don't know if you can imagine what it's like to be hit by a crocus bulb that's traveling 98 miles per hour, but this poor kid caught the first one above the left temple and crumpled. It took some dozen men from heavy appliances to finally restrain my husband from further violence. But again, when these guys found out that this was *Mark Leyner,* it was all high-fives and autographs—forget about the kid, who's propped up unconscious against a 50-pound bag of peat moss.

"It seemed like another lifetime when Mark and I would lie in bed at night reading *Bleak House* and *The Spoils of Poynton* to each other. More recently he'd insist on regaling me with the most vile, adolescent, fetishistic sorts of trash as I lay there with the covers pulled over my face. Just to give you a random example of the type of bedtime story I was subjected to, here's the jacket copy from a typical offering:

> She pulled Snap's pants off and tossed them on the floor.
> "What are these?" she asked, her hand probing between his legs.
> "Balls . . . t-t-testicles," he stammered.
> "They look good," she said, brandishing a straight-edge razor that glinted as she began to sharpen it on a long leather strop.

> From the day that he got his first Polaroid camera, Snap was the quintessential all-American shutterbug—Cub Scout photo club, high school newspaper photography editor, U.P.I. stringer. But when he went 200 miles beneath the surface of the earth to get photos of a flesh-eating, gynecocratic, subterranean culture, his life began to go out of focus and he had to pull out all the f-stops just to survive!

"I'd make one final attempt at persuading Mark to hospitalize himself and begin long-term in-patient psychotherapy. I arranged to meet him at one of his preferred haunts, in the hopes that a congenial environment would make him, if not wholly sympathetic, at least somewhat receptive to my recommendation. It was a South Philadelphia after-hours club frequented by a nefarious assortment of methamphetamine traffickers, Cosa Nostra hitmen, extortionists, bookmakers, and Bryn Mawr students who found the truculent, garishly garbed habitués of this lurid night spot a perfect libidinal antidote to their professors—whose repertoire of facial tics, speech impediments, halitosis, and dandruff (which clogged the wide wales of their corduroy jackets) made the Oresteian trilogy and Isthmian odes so insufferable.

"I told him that it had all became more than I could bear: the insane obsession with his body, with compulsively altering the size and shape of its parts, with its secretions and their

sundry smells and tastes; the government's punitive consfis-
cation program that was dispossessing us of everything we'd
worked so hard to acquire; the pills, the booze, the Bolasterone, and testosterone cypionate; the philandering; and most of
all—the strident, evangelical exaltation of his own psychopa-
thology, as if there were some revelatory alchemical truth in
his stunted development, ordaining him to proselytize a be-
nighted humanity.

"He stared vacantly past me, sucking on the silver skull
he wore on a chain around his neck, looked at his wrist-
watch, and mumbled something about having to meet a
new business partner with whom he was purchasing a syn-
dicate of decrepit nursing homes.

"And that was the end."

THE CONTESTANT: What is an excerpt from Arleen Portada's
*When Telling Your Husband That He's "A Delusional, Narcissistic
Sadist with Deep-Seated, Unresolved Issues About His Mother" Just
Isn't Enough Anymore: My Seven Turbulent Years as the Wife of Cult
Author Mark Leyner?*

THE HOST: That's absolutely correct, for $25,000! And we're
all out of time for today! See you back here tomorrow!!

THE AUDIENCE: [Wild cheering]

THE PRERECORDED VOICE: A tintinnabulation of kisses deep
in the brain. A tiny leak of neurotransmitters, perhaps. An infinitesimal burst gasket in the latticework of cerebral piping. But
the densely packed, intricately knotted ribbons of self-
congratulatory cognition writhe into perpetuity . . . into the
perpetuity of night.

[Roll credits]

[Dissolve]

WHERE THE BEE SUCKS, THERE SUCK I

"In your culture, it's not considered appropriate for a heterosexual man to be in the presence of his heterosexual sister if she is naked, correct?" asked the anthropologist.

The tribal headman nodded. "Yes."

The anthropologist, who was tape-recording the conversation and taking written notes, made a quick notation and then looked up, smiling at the headman.

"It is also not considered appropriate for a heterosexual woman to be in the presence of her heterosexual brother if he is naked, correct?"

"Correct."

"Why is this?"

"The modesty of a man or a woman in the presence of his or her opposite-sex sibling is a built-in preventative mechanism that has the effect of precluding sexual arousal. Sexual arousal between siblings is incestuous and incest is an absolute taboo in our culture."

"What about a homosexual man and his heterosexual sister?"

"The heterosexual sister will feel ashamed to be naked in front of her homosexual brother."

"But the homosexual brother will not be aroused by the nakedness of his sister."

"Presumably not."

"So what's the problem?"

"The heterosexual sister may herself become aroused by exhibiting her naked body to a man—whether or not he is aroused—and since in this case the man is her brother, the arousal is incestuous and taboo."

"That makes sense."

The anthropologist bowed and grunted, a sign of respect.

The headman bowed and grunted reciprocally.

"What about two brothers—can they see each other naked?"

"Yes."

"And two sisters can see each other naked, too?"

"Of course. Same-sex siblings often see each other naked. They frequently shower in each other's presence and try clothes on in each other's presence, etc."

"What if a homosexual man is in the presence of his heterosexual brother who is naked? Wouldn't it be possible for the homosexual man to become aroused by the naked body of his brother?"

The headman stared far into the distance without answering. He gazed out toward the great mountains where the sacred ancestral burial places were.

The anthropologist jotted something down in his notebook and continued his questioning.

"And what about a naked homosexual woman and her homosexual sister who is naked, or two naked homosexual brothers? Wouldn't the opportunities for incestuous arousal be exponentially increased in these instances? And yet there is no taboo against two sisters being naked together whatever their sexual orientations are and there's no taboo against two naked brothers in each other's presence no matter what their sexual orientations are. Can you explain this to me?"

The headman beckoned to several of his underlings and whispered something to them.

He said: "Take the anthropologist into the woods and kill him. If anyone from the village wants to eat his flesh, let them. I'm not into it, but I have no problem with anyone who is. Just get him out of my sight and into the woods and slaughter him as you would a wild pig or a tapir. He's really beginning to annoy me! Go! Take him!"

"Yes." The young acolytes nodded, bowing and grunting.

Off they went, escorting the scribbling anthropologist into the jungle.

"OK, who's next?" asked the tribal headman.

His administrative assistant ran an index finger down a clipboard. "Your three o'clock is Ralph Korngold—he's vice-president in charge of sales and marketing for Genitotech, a specialized biotechnology company located in Sparta, New Jersey."

"Where's New Jersey?"

The administrative assistant pointed beyond the great mountains where the sacred ancestral burial places were.

"Show him in," said the headman, straightening the cartridge bandoliers that crisscrossed his bare chest.

The Genitotech VP, sweating in a blue double-breasted suit, entered the pavilion, bowed and grunted.

"Korngold, what can I do for you?" asked the headman.

"Chief, I don't know how familiar you are with the Genitotech Company and its flagship product, Phallotropin . . ."

"Phallotropin—if I'm not mistaken—is a patented form of synthetic penile growth hormone (PGH). The drug was originally developed as an otological drop to facilitate ear wax removal. Then, a number of men who inadvertently ingested the solution orally began to notice significant penile growth. In subsequent FDA trials, synthetic PGH was credited with adding up to six inches of penile length to men who produced insufficient quantities of the hormone on their own. Phallotropin, along with Upjohn's Rogaine and Johnson and Johnson's Retin-A, is a golden product of pharmaceutical serendipity, a drug that was originally developed for one very specific usage and which later manifested a quite unexpected and much more lucrative indication. Researchers at Genitotech have 'fine-tuned' the drug to work gradually so there's no sudden bulge, an important benefit emphasized in Genitotech's new television commercials ("People at the office noticed that I was looking younger, more virile—but they couldn't quite put their finger on exactly what it was"). I also know that the writer Mark Leyner has supposedly signed a multimillion-dollar contract to be the spokesperson for Phallotropin."

"That's amazing! How is it that you're so well versed in the developmental history of Phallotropin?"

"Look, just because we're an extremely isolated, hallucinogen-snorting tribe of headhunters doesn't mean that we don't read the trade journals . . . *Urology Today, Annals of Endocrinology*, etc. Granted, we get them pretty late—the November issue of *Urology Today*, for instance, didn't get here until May—but we read them. But anyway, Korngold, why'd you come all the way down here to talk to me about Phallotropin? At the risk of sounding chauvinistic, our men are more than adequately endowed."

"Chief, I don't know how closely you follow American pop culture. . . ."

The headman shrugged. "I know Sting, 'cause he's down here a lot. But otherwise, by the time we get *People* or *Entertainment Weekly*, whoever they're talking about is usually dead and buried."

"Well, let me fill you in. Leyner was originally going to be the Phallotropin Man. He was perfect—a huge reputation for his books and hyper-macho image, especially with our targeted consumer sector, the adolescent male. He'd even experimented with some amateur genital enhancement as a youngster. But the guy's run into some major problems lately."

"The Lincoln's morning breath thing . . . with the punitive confiscation?"

"That and an ugly divorce and defections that have decimated almost the entirety of his upper-echelon staff, and there are rumors of bizarre behavior—episodes of extreme delusional megalomania alternating with bouts of hysterical paranoia and deep depression, alcohol and Percodan abuse, etc. etc. And we just couldn't take the risk with a product like this—Genitotech expects to sell over $650 million of Phallotropin in its first year on the market."

"Mamma mia!" exclaimed the headman.

"The long and the short of it, Chief, is that we've dropped Leyner and we'd like you to be the Phallotropin Man."

The headman cupped a hand over his mouth and cogitated for a long while.

"What about side effects . . . ?" he asked finally. "I don't want to bring ignominy upon my tribe by endorsing a product that's unsafe."

"Not to worry, Chief. So far as we've been able to determine, Phallotropin's only side effects are hirsutism, priapism, and Holmes-Berle disease—a rare form of dementia caused by burrowing microworms that live in the brain."

"And I'd get the same seven-figure deal that Leyner got?"

"Same cash deal, incredible media exposure for you and your tribe, and enough free Phallotropin to make you guys the preeminent studs of the Amazon. What do you say?"

"Korngold, I'm going to go snort some ebene, stagger around wild-eyed for a while with green mucus streaming from my nostrils, leave my body, descend to the subterranean world, evaluate your proposal with my dead ancestors, and then get back to you."

"What sort of time frame are we talking about here?" Korngold asked, checking his appointment book.

"We're talking a day or two, three tops."

The headman stood, bowed, and grunted.

Korngold did likewise. "Chief, I'm looking forward to your

decision and hopefully to a long and prosperous partnership with the Genitotech Company."

The young acolytes reappeared, rooting their molars with long toothpicks, and escorted the stocky biotech exec into the rain forest.

The headman flicked a pebble at his administrative assistant, who'd been staring off into space, scratching his crotch. The round stone glanced sharply off his forehead.

"Who's next, *babaçú heto-hoká* [worthless one]?"

"Chief, a Mr. Geoffrey Hoag and a Ms. Pamela van Zandt of Pretty Polly Inc., a British hosiery producer, were supposed to have been here half an hour ago. Maybe they're lost."

"Maybe . . ." echoed the headman bemusedly, gazing out toward a clearing in the jungle where a jaguar, who'd eaten the 50 pounds of rugelach that Korngold had brought for the chief, lay sprawled among white bakery boxes and string, immobile, his belly extremely fat, panting in the heat.

YELLOW FEVER

Ashley had just eaten the last chocolate egg.

"Mama, whatever possessed Mia Farrow to marry Frank Sinatra?" she asked, her words slurred somewhat by the thick volume of confection filling her little mouth and encumbering the agility of that trilling little tongue.

"Dear, not another word until you swallow what's in your mouth. You're a very naughty, very gluttonous little sugar addict."

Ashley, with visible effort, swallowed the large sweet bolus, quite prematurely, especially as she was accustomed to savoring her chocolate upon her palate until it had seemed to melt away.

"That's better. Now, what makes you ask why Mia Farrow would marry Frank Sinatra?"

"Well, Mama, when I look at the other men in Mia's life—sensitive, artistic men like Andre Previn and Woody Allen—I just can't understand what she saw in such a coarse, vulgar man who flaunted his Mafia connections and referred to women as 'broads' and 'cunts.'"

Ashley reached into a crystal wassail bowl filled with jellybeans and candy corn and conveyed a fistful to her mouth.

"Ashley!"

"I'm sorry, Mama," she mumbled. "These are my last ones, I promise."

"They most certainly are, young lady. Why, if you keep this up, you'll be the only little girl in Gregory Day School wearing dentures."

"Last ones, promise."

"Ashley, what I don't think you understand quite yet is that in their heart of hearts, women don't lust after men who are merely sensitive and artistic. Men like that are ultimately quite boring. On the other hand, women can't truly be loved and nurtured by men who are brutes and nothing more. And often in the course of a woman's life, she vacillates back and forth from one extreme to the other in an effort to satisfy the spectrum of her needs. How rare it is that a single man can embody both of these seemingly antipodal profiles. Your grandfather, Ashley, was such a man."

"Grandpa Mark?"

"Yes, Grandpa Mark—may his soul rest in peace."

"Mama, what sort of man was Grandpa Mark?" Ashley asked, stealthily plucking several caramels from a jar across the table, as her mother took a tissue and dabbed her eyes, which had moistened at this recollection of her late, illustrious father.

"Your Grandpa Mark was a violent maverick loner with a fatal weakness for Hispanic women . . . and he was the finest, most audacious, most illuminating, most influential and imitated writer of his time. He was all these things."

"Will there ever be anyone like him again, Mama?"

"Never."

I was awakened by the gentle caress of a familiar flipper-like appendage.

"Oh . . . Joe . . . I just had the weirdest dream. I was dead, I guess, and I had this granddaughter on a perpetual sucrose binge and . . ."

"Mr. Leyner, I'm leaving."

"Wake me up when you get back, OK, Joe?"

"No, Mr. Leyner. I mean I'm *leaving.* I'm quitting."

I discerned through groggy eyes Joe's luggage in the doorway.

"Et tu, babe?" I said.

"I'm so sorry, Mr. Leyner. But I just can't handle it any-more. . . ."

"Forget about it, Joe. Do what you have to do. And if you ever need a reference . . ."

The image of yeoman Joe Casale struggling with his suitcases as he made his way down the hall dissolved in a mist of emotion.

I loved that guy.

ZWANGSWIRTSCHAFT

On September 24, 1994, federal operatives, acting under the authority of the Punitive Confiscation Act, seized Chapter Five manuscript entries for the letters B, E, H, J, K, L, N, O, P, Q, R, U, and X.

Team Leyner deeply regrets the impossibility of including these sections in what the author had intended to be a complete abecedarian series.

CHAPTER SIX

AN ORAL HISTORY

CONNIE CHUNG: I'm fairly certain that I was the last one to see him on that final day. He was in the throes of his work—writing frenetically, wearing his trough. (So that he never had to leave his computer keyboard, he'd devised a small trough that hung from his neck and from which he ate continuously while he typed.)

Whether it was tragedy or comedy that he'd been commissioned to produce, the sine qua non was elegance. The apotheosis of elegance and élan in his own rough-hewn attire and phlegmatic demeanor, he had written extensively on the subject, including a 1,300-page disquisition on armpit fetishism composed in the form of intricate commentaries on the hitherto suppressed Polaroid photographs of Bruce Lee's underarms that were taken by Steve McQueen in the late 1960s when the two were scouting locations in Bangkok for a Kung Fu version of J. D. Salinger's *The Catcher in the Rye*—a film that was never made. (I might add here that McQueen's other dream project, *Honey, I Shrunk the Children of a Lesser God,* the story of a maniacal scientist obsessed with miniaturizing deaf children, was also never made.)

Incessantly haunted by hallucinations of apocalyptic mayhem and driven half-mad by a desire to simultaneously terrorize and seduce women in uniform, he has attempted to live a decent, productive life. To those whom he has offended, those who have found his almost masturbatory exaltations of Darwinian natural selection cynical and misanthropic, I offer the following incident from his youth as he himself recounts it in his shocking memoir, *Et Tu, Babe*:

> As the anesthesia wore off, a bushy-haired man in a gauze mask, with a stethoscope around his neck, and a percussion hammer and sphygmomanometer jutting from the pocket of his white lab coat, came into focus.
>
> "What's your name?" he asked.
>
> "Leyner. Mark Leyner," I answered groggily.
>
> "Do you know where you are?"
>
> "All I know is that I answered an ad in *High Times* for volunteers for experimental brain surgery and that a week later a Nissan mini-van picked me up and I was driven blindfolded to a secret laboratory in Tijuana."
>
> "You don't remember undergoing the procedure?"
>
> "Procedure? What are you talking—?"
>
> At that moment, half a dozen FDA agents, automatic weapons blazing, killed the "doctor" who had operated on me, and then escorted me to the border where I was given $20 and a small bottle of effervescent apple juice.

JOAN JETT: Notwithstanding all the bullshit to the contrary, I was the last person to be with Mark Leyner before he disappeared. I remember that afternoon vividly—Mark was at his escritoire, his fingers a blur across the keyboard of his laptop, thick daubs of chili paste on his temples, his nipples, and his balls. {Leyner would apply a poultice of chili paste to his temples, nipples, and testicles whenever he felt "blocked," claiming that it unclogged the channels through which his "interior elixir" flowed.}

He was his usual confident, ebulliently bellicose self, with his sights set very much on the future. For instance, while I was there that day, he'd occasionally—as a momentary respite from his literary labors—devote his attention to a linen design he was working on for J. P. Stevens' "Team Leyner Bed and Bath Collection." {The flat and fitted sheets depicted four 275-pound Nigerian infantrymen bathing naked in a sylvan pond, their uniforms and weapons hanging from the branches of a spreading sycamore tree. The pillowcases were a canary legal-pad print, emblazoned with miscellaneous "numerical fun facts" rendered in Leyner's exuberantly juvenile calligraphy—e.g., "There are 40 million denture wearers in the United States," "Bats roosting under the Congress Avenue Bridge in downtown Austin eat 14 tons of insects a night," "Creutzfeldt-Jakob disease (a form of spongiform encephalopathy) strikes one person in a million worldwide," etc.]

Later on in the afternoon, we took a couple of bottles of scotch up to the rooftop patio and we played this drinking game that Mark invented. You listen to one of those talk-radio stations and every time you hear the word "the" or "and" you have to take a drink.

I remember . . . that afternoon, we . . . we . . . I'm sorry . . . I get kind of emotional when I . . . Do you have a tissue? I just really miss that son of a bitch. If you can imagine being kidnapped by some gorgeous psychopath and you're in this stolen semi, and each tire is inflated with laughing gas, and you're plummeting down this endless gradient, and he's not saying a word, but there's this . . . this peripheral blur of subliminal billboards . . . and it's the most beautiful spaced-out erotic poetry in the world, and it's *his* poetry, and it's speaking to you in this incredible way that every woman yearns to be spoken to, and . . . well, that's what it was like being with Mark Leyner. He was real intense.

GEORGE PLIMPTON: Leyner didn't have a regular shower head in his shower—he'd attached one of those Water-Piks that people use for cleaning their teeth. He liked an extremely concentrated, piercing stream of water in which to bathe. He found it more effective in dislodging dirt from those hard-to-clean parts of his body—all the furrows and crevices—and, frankly, I think he just liked the way it felt. Sometimes he'd lie prostrate in the tub for hours letting this thin pulsing line of hot water hit the top of his coccyx bone—the area from which his vestigial tail was removed soon after his foster father found him on the Pebble Beach golf course.

His foster dad was an avid golfer, and one afternoon he was out on the back nine and he hit a wedge shot and carved a hefty divot out of the fairway, and there—unearthed and wriggling in the sun for the first time in its life—was a cute itsy-bitsy little fetal humanoid whose biological mother had, just moments before, buried it alive. That was Mark Leyner! The poor little . . . Do you have a tissue? [Leyner's natural mother had suffered accidental gamma ray exposure as a teenager. Doctors warned her that there was a possibility that the radiation had scrambled the DNA in her eggs, dooming her to mutant births. Dr. Shlomo Hemplemann, noted forensic psychiatrist and author of *One Monster, Many Mommies: Whose Fault Is Mark Leyner?*, contends that overwhelming anxiety concerning the potential abnormality of the newborn motivated this attempted infanticide.]

From these humble beginnings to international superstardom to his current contretemps—a fascinating and complex journey. I've come to know hundreds of artists in my life, but I must say that I've never encountered a single one—writer, painter, composer—possessed by anything approaching the colossal scope of Leyner's ambition. I remember sitting with him on a marble bench sipping local grappa under an old pomegranate tree in a beautiful little courtyard on the Lou Ferrigno estate, and I asked him what he hoped to ultimately accomplish in his career. He talked about his vision of a nation where every home has a speaker that broadcasts passages from his books throughout waking hours, where his texts are read over loudspeakers on the main streets.

CARL SAGAN: He was absolutely serious about leaving Earth and relocating elsewhere. He was not at all nostalgic about the terrestrial world, and he was quite unsympathetic and impatient with my ecological concerns. He'd say, "Carl, the world's population is putting such a strain on the global infrastructure and, in particular, on the world's water supply and sewerage capacities, that by the middle of the twenty-first century, if someone flushes a toilet in Mombasa and you're in the shower in San Diego, you'll get scalded. All the more reason to get off the planet, babe. Why stay if conditions are going to be so impossible? Rather than flagellating ourselves for having plundered the earth of its precious resources and for having toxified the globe's air, water, and soil, why not channel our intellectual and spiritual energies into figuring out how to get the hell out of here. Once we're a safe distance from this place, on a nice hospitable planet with a respirable atmosphere and fauna capable of being ground up into some kind of burger, then we can determine culpability and mete out the punishment."

There are still so many things we don't understand about him—even those of us who know him well. Why, for instance, did he write a weekly letter to General Hideki Tojo, Japan's wartime prime minister who was hanged in 1948 as a war criminal? [These bizarre missives—each of which was returned unopened and peppered with the Japanese postal service's "Return to Sender" stamp, and dutifully filed and cataloged in a vault in the catacombs of the Team Leyner Library by Team Leyner archivist Yvette Bokassa—were no hastily scribbled apostrophes, but lengthy, detailed, searingly self-appraising synopses and analyses of that week's events, often running in excess of 75 single-spaced pages!] Why correspond with an infamous Japanese general who's been dead for over half a century? Why?

I was on my way to Sea World in a rented Ford Escort, blow-drying my bangs, when the news came over the radio that he'd disappeared. I had to pull over.

CHRISTIAAN BARNARD: When Leyner made the decision to have the mole in his right eyebrow removed, the news was apparently leaked to several fanzines. Apprised of the impending surgery, his followers immediately began clamoring for the mole—as evidenced by the thousands upon thousands of phone calls and letters received at headquarters, his fans wanted that mole and they wanted it bad.

Team Leyner elected to sponsor a lottery, the winner of which would actually receive the mole in a transplant. The mole would be grafted onto any part of the winner's body that he or she chose. I was personally recruited by Leyner himself to perform the mole transplant. The winner of the lottery was a sixteen-year-old girl from Terre Haute, Indiana, who sent in her high school yearbook picture with an arrow drawn indicating the center of her forehead.

After I excised the mole from Leyner's eyebrow, it was frozen and flown by helicopter to University Hospital in Terre Haute, where I performed the procedure. Tragically, the recipient died four days later.

A typical mole is a collection of cells that contain an unusually high concentration of melanin. Leyner's mole not only contained high concentrations of melanin, but staggeringly high concentrations of Hexalone, Bolasterone, and Dehydralone—powerful anabolic steroids, *plus* significant levels of cesium 137 and strontium 90.

By the second day following the transplant, the mole had almost completely subsumed the girl. The only vestige of her that remained visible amid the throbbing brown neoplasm was the big toe of her left foot, which she could still wiggle in response to questions.

I asked her: "After all that's happened to you, do you still idolize Leyner, do you still consider him some sort of messianic savior?"

"Yes! Yes!" She wiggled emphatically.

I'll never forget that fuchsia toenail twitching zealously, as her EEG became flatter and flatter. . . .

CHIP GIBSON: Let's go back to 1983 or 1984. I'm fuckin' selling stolen $5,000 Chanel quilted leather biker jackets out of the trunk of my car for $600 a pop. And I'm bangin' this manicurist on weekends—fuckin' bangin' her in a hot tub at a friend's condo in Fort Lee, New Jersey, and I'm drivin' at the time a fuckin' . . . a fuckin' . . . uh . . . a fuckin' . . . what the hell was that called . . . a fuckin' . . . fuckin' uh . . . Toyota Celica GT. Red. And I got this air freshener on my rearview mirror— you send a photograph of yourself to this company in Florida and they make an air freshener out of it—so I got this little cutout of myself dangling from my rearview mirror and it smells like a fuckin' coconut. And this broad's got a big fuckin' brown recluse spider bite scar on her ass . . .

You want "oral history"? I can fuckin' go back to 1958, for Christ's sake. There I am, I'm in the doctor's office, I'm fuckin' five years old. My parents take me to this doctor to see why I talk like this. 'Cause, see, my parents don't talk like this. My father's a pretty well-known anthropologist at Yale—he's pretty famous for translating the hieroglyphs from the fuckin' . . . the fuckin' . . . who the fuck . . . they're like the earliest fuckin' wetbacks . . . the fuckin' . . . the Mayans. The Mayans. And my mother was like head of the Brandeis Alumni Association, y'know, nationwide. So they don't know why I talk like this and they take me to this specialist. And we're sittin' there. And I remember I'm eatin' a fuckin' corn muffin and I'm hittin' the doctor on the side of the head with the back of my hand while I'm talkin' to him like whap! c'mon, you stupid prick, what's your fuckin' problem? and I'm sprayin' corn muffin in the guy's face, I'm like pollinating this fuckin' guy with these yellow crumbs and I'm like whap! whap! y'know? 'Cause I hate this guy, I hate this

prick. And he says to my parents: I don't think there's any neurological damage, maybe he should see a speech therapist. And I'm
like fuckin': don't quit your day job, Doc. Whap! Whap!

At any rate, I did eventually see a speech therapist, and in
1990 I became Associate Publisher and Division Vice-
President at the Crown Publishing Group, and that's how I
originally met Mark Leyner.

Leyner's recent problems, beginning with the Lincoln's
morning breath theft and culminating with his disappearance,
disrupted the most elaborate, energetic, and expensive sales
and marketing program we at Crown had ever undertaken for
any author. Since Leyner had his own Saturday morning
cartoon show and a Leyner doll, Crown had secured a deal
with Toys "R" Us to sell his books in the toy stores next to
the dolls. One of the most exciting things about the project
for Crown was that—with Toys "R" Us—we had the
opportunity to reach a subteen group, giving us a whole new
market. Then we signed a fifteen-year deal with Mattel to sell
a line of Team Leyner preschool and infant toys based on
characters from Leyner's books. There was a cuddly little
stuffed "Carmella," a "Joe Casale" tub toy with movable
flippers, a "Kid Woman" talking doll that spoke Spanish or
Quechua depending on which braid you pulled, bionic elderly
bodyguard "action figures"—we anticipated annual sales of
close to $200 million. But now the entire marketing program
is on what's called "permanent hiatus." It's a shame.

I like Leyner personally—he's a hell of a lot of fun to party
with—but I don't think he's ever considered how many people
are hurt by his irresponsible behavior. And I don't think it's
going to be a very "Team Leyner" Christmas for all the folks
we're going to have to lay off. . . .

[The announcement of Leyner's disappearance sent Mattel
stock plunging on the New York Stock Exchange to $35.625

a share, down $8.075. The news also sent shock waves through the Tokyo Stock Exchange. At the midday recess, the Nikkei index of 225 issues was down 6,574.75 points, or about 15 percent, to 24,115.79.]

JUSTICE CLARENCE THOMAS: On a number of occasions, on the way home from the Supreme Court, I stopped in at Team Leyner Headquarters for a Coke or a Bud Light—but it was no matter of great import . . .

SENATOR CECIL VALGUS: Justice Thomas, approximately how many times did you stop in at Team Leyner on the way home from the Supreme Court?

JUSTICE CLARENCE THOMAS: Senator, I'd say approximately 1,100 times I stopped in at Team Leyner—and in order to continue a debate I'd been having with Mark about, say, the relationship between quantum mechanics and artificial intelligence or St. Augustine's conception of a neo-Platonic God or Lacanian psychoanalysis—I'd stop in at Team Leyner Headquarters and have a Diet Dr. Pepper or an Amstel Light.

SENATOR CECIL VALGUS: Justice Thomas, did you ever—on any of these approximately 1,100 occasions when you say you stopped in at Team Leyner Headquarters to continue a discussion—take anabolic steroids, Thorazine, Percodan, or LSD with Mark Leyner?

JUSTICE CLARENCE THOMAS: Senator, I categorically deny that. I did, on several occasions, stop in at Team Leyner Headquarters on the way home from the Supreme Court to continue a discussion I might be having with Mark about the sonnets of Gerard de Nerval or the impact of movable type and gunpowder on the decline of the feudal nobility, and I did on a number of those occasions have several tablespoons of Maalox Extra-strength Antacid/Antiflatulent and several Extra-strength Tylenol Gelcaps.

SENATOR CECIL VALGUS: Justice Thomas, did Mark Leyner ever discuss with you his desire to develop a clandestine nuclear weapons plant at the Team Leyner facility?

JUSTICE CLARENCE THOMAS: No, Senator.

SENATOR CECIL VALGUS: More specifically, Justice Thomas, did he ever discuss with you using funds from a secret family trust in Liechtenstein to acquire the technology to produce weapons-grade plutonium?

JUSTICE CLARENCE THOMAS: Senator, that is absolutely, categorically untrue. Nothing even remotely resembling such a conversation ever took place between Mark Leyner and myself.

SENATOR CECIL VALGUS: Mr. Chairman, I have no further questions for Justice Thomas.

JUSTICE CLARENCE THOMAS: Mr. Chairman, with all due respect to the members of this committee, I must express to you my belief that conducting these investigations into the activities of Team Leyner at a time when Mr. Leyner is unable to participate and unable to refute the scurrilous attacks on his name—at a time when his whereabouts are unknown and his well-being, his very existence, is in doubt—is profoundly unfair, and it's tearing the very fabric of our society asunder.

DIANE VON FURSTENBERG: I was the last person to be alone with him before he vanished that afternoon. He was dressed in a green uniform with gold epaulets, crotchless blue pantaloons, and red top boots, unshaven, bleary-eyed, working relentlessly— mauling his computer keyboard like some kind of rabid animal— pausing intermittently to gobble a handful of electric-eel roe from a nearby terrine, wiping his mouth on a piece of fan mail, and then renewing his assault. I don't know how graphic you want me to get—but it was obvious that he was extremely aroused by whatever he was writing. And there was just something so incredibly sexy about him as he worked. He was so . . . he just had this . . . this "thing" about him.

Just to give you another example—I remember a couple of years ago, Mark was in Paris to have some sort of surgery, and, in the middle of the operation, the guy gets up off the operating table, walks out of the hospital, and strolls into the Yves Saint Laurent spring couture show, onto the runway, viscera bulging out of an eight-inch abdominal incision, clamps and hemostats and catheters dangling from his body. And the girls—the Christy Turlingtons, the Linda Evangelistas, the Naomi Campbells—they were all over him! And sure enough, that spring, you'd go to a dinner party or a gala and you'd actually see women wearing priceless couture ensembles that had been artistically stained with iodine germicidal scrub and adorned with a variety of silver surgical instruments—that's how charismatic a presence he was, and that's how pervasive his influence was among people who wanted to be irreproachably au courant.

HAROLD PINTER: I admire Leyner tremendously. First of all, his work—stunning, magnificent! His play *Varicose Moon* is achingly beautiful. I think it will be unnecessary for playwrights to write any new plays for some time now—*Varicose Moon* should suffice. In fact, I think it would be vulgar for playwrights to burden the public with their offerings given the creation of this coruscating masterwork.

He has also been a wise and magnanimous friend. It was Leyner who first introduced me to Beckett's Hawaiian writing—and for that alone, I remain eternally indebted to him. [Between the completion of his novel *The Unnameable* and his debut as a dramatist with *En attendant Godot,* Samuel Beckett, desperate for money to support the child he'd fathered with American singer Kate Smith, moved to Hawaii and secured a job in public relations, writing brochure copy for the Hyatt Regency Hotel on Maui. Long suppressed by the Beckett estate, which publicly denied their existence, Beckett's Maui brochures constitute a fascinating lens through which readers can further explore the mind of the angst-ridden Nobel Laureate. Today, many Beckett scholars consider these brochures (which hype the hotel's 750,000-gallon pool with its romantic grotto, 130-foot water slide, and swim-up cocktail bar, championship golf course, lei-making and ukelele classes, and authentic luau) Beckett's most important work.]

Here's a wonderful instance of Leyner's intellectual generosity. I was working on a play, a play that contained all of my characteristic motifs—the fallibility of memory, the ultimate unknowability of women to men and men to women, the notion that all human contact is battle—in oblique, elliptical dialogue delivered by an estranged elderly couple who remain immobile for most of the play. And I just was not happy with it at all. So I gave the script to Leyner. He took it with him to his hotel that evening, and later that same night, he rang me up and suggested that instead of the action taking place in a house in London's Hampstead Heath, as I'd intended, it take place in Reno, Nevada, at the Eldorado Hotel. It's been discovered that some six metric tons of an experimental, highly mutagenic fungus developed by the Defense Department's Advanced Fungal Weapons Research Center, located in nearby Sparks, have seeped into the city's underlying aquifer. As the play opens, scientists suspect the lethal fungus of having rapidly evolved into a sophisticated ratiocinative being capable of defeating all but the top two or three chess grandmasters in the world. Well, it was an astonishingly brilliant suggestion—it would never have occurred to me in a million years! It totally transformed the play, which critics would laud as the most powerful and innovative of my career.

KATARINA WITT: It's been over two years since I spent that final afternoon alone with him as he furiously endeavored to complete his memoirs, and yet I still find him as maddeningly seductive and utterly unfathomable a man as ever. I don't think a half-hour goes by in the course of a day when I don't catch myself fantasizing about him.

I recently competed in the World Figure Skating Championships in Stuttgart. It was the climax of my program, I was doing a triple Salchow and, right in the middle, in midair, I just left my body and there I was with Mark again—this was during the most important international competition of the year! Well, it turns out that, in my disembodied state, I didn't do a triple Salchow, I did a septuagesimal Salchow—that's seventy rotations in the air!—obviously a feat that had never been accomplished before and has not been since. My coach, who'd always been a bit superstitious, saw the devil's work in the freak Salchow, and she quit and entered a monastic order in Baden-Baden.

DR. GEORGE NICHOPOULOS: Substance abuse problem? In my medical opinion, no. He'd been putting a tremendous amount of pressure on himself to finish this particular book before, what he called, "an imminent siege by the spineless degenerates arrayed against me."

If I prescribed Percodan, Demerol, Valium, Quaaludes, Placidyl, pentobarbital, Anadrol, Primobolan, erythropoeitin, amineptine, and clenbuterol for him, it was simply to ease his mind and give him some enhanced stamina. Like I said, there was the pressure of this book and the pressure of just being who he was.

RON HOWARD: Gosh . . . what can one say about *"Le Leyner"*? I just hope that the Team Leyner sign in Times Square isn't taken down. To me, that sign is synonymous with New York City. It *is* New York City—it's brash, it's ballsy, it's like "Yo!" [The huge neon Team Leyner sign at 2 Times Square simulates positron emission tomography images of Leyner's brain function as he writes, laid over a magnetic resonance image of his brain anatomy—so pedestrians below can actually observe glucose metabolism at various sites within Leyner's cerebral cortex as he's producing one of his critically acclaimed best-sellers. The 85-ton, 105-foot-high, 61-foot-wide sign, built at a cost exceeding $5 million, features nearly 70 miles of fiber-optic tubing, more than eight miles of neon tubing, and more than 34,000 light bulbs.]

Actually, you know what I'd do with the Team Leyner sign? I'd put it into orbit, so it could be like the earth's Statue of Liberty—so it would be the first logo of humanity that the extraterrestrial aliens see when they immigrate here.

Come to think of it, there is one personal experience that stands out in my mind when I think about him. I was with a group of Hollywood directors and actors on a sightseeing bus tour of Team Leyner Headquarters. Leyner happened to be on the grounds that afternoon—he was doing some kind of martial arts sparring with one of his elderly bodyguards—and he recognized me and invited me in for iced tea. While I was there, a UPS truck pulled up to the front entrance and the driver unloaded a calutron. [A calutron is a device that produces highly enriched weapons-grade uranium through a process called electromagnetic isotope separation.] Leyner signed for the merchandise and sat back down with me, making no mention of the delivery. I recognized the Chinese ideogram for "This Side Up" so I'm fairly certain that it was either from Taiwan or the People's Republic. About a half-hour later, another UPS truck pulls up, and the driver unloads a shipment of zirconium from an export company in Frankfurt. [Zirconium can be used to make uranium fuel rods.] Again, Leyner signed for the delivery, returned to finish his drink, and then vanished. I was allowed a last swallow of tea and then escorted back to the bus by one of his minions. Weird, huh? Weird guy, though. But fun weird. I don't know if other men had this experience, but Leyner made me feel really small physically, really stupid, and really sexually inadequate. But it was still so cool being with him! [Though accurate intelligence is sketchy, Defense Department experts say they believe Leyner was probably two to five years away from producing a crude nuclear weapon.]

JESSICA HAHN: I'll tell you what I've been telling everybody all along: I was *the* last person to be with Mark Leyner before he disappeared. *Fact.* OK? And I've offered to take a polygraph. I don't hear any of these bogus last-to-be-with-Leyner wannabes from "Nightline" and "Larry King" offering to take a lie detector test, do you? If you had polygraph equipment here in the van, I'd take the goddamn test right now. I was the last one to see him—that's the truth.

This is from my diary entry for that day: "He was haunted by a ceaseless ambition and a deep loneliness that he hoped fame and an ostentatiously vulgar lifestyle would alleviate. He promised me that someday we'd make love for thirteen straight hours in Death Valley, and we'd sweat so much that we'd end up skeletons—two grinning skeletons, pumping and rattling under the red thermonuclear sun. If only that were possible now . . ."

Mark had been tutoring me in creative writing. I'd never had that much confidence in my ability to express myself, but Mark really made me feel as if I had a natural aptitude for verse. Here's a poem I wrote—after a couple of lessons with Mark—describing one of the gardens at Team Leyner Headquarters. The part at the end about the mule is a sort of imaginative embellishment: "Innumerable shades of green./An infinite taxonomy of greenness/trebled by the effects of direct, deflected, and umbral sunlight./The ambient "contrast" modulated by the evanescing day./Each leaf in sovereign motion,/yet all according in synchronous oscillation—/from branch to tree to copse./Flies wheel above/compoundly eyeing the furfuraceous eczema that covers/the buttocks of a moribund mule."

I know that during that last afternoon, he got a dirty phone call from Camille Paglia. It was on the speaker phone, so I heard most of it. It was pretty explicit. I know I heard the words "tart mucosity." It sort of faded in and out, so I figured she was calling from her car phone and going under trestles. Mark didn't seem to mind the call, though. But I don't think he was really paying attention.

And suddenly headquarters was illuminated by arc lights, and surrounded by heavily armed officers in flak jackets, and hundreds of riot troops and sharpshooters from the Punitive Confiscation Tactical Division.

He was wearing Hugo Boss moss-green suede pajama bottoms. He had reached the climactic section of his Team Leyner memoirs, and he was typing like a lunatic, flailing at his keyboard in ecstasy like some enraptured pentacostal organist.

He was in mid-sentence when they wrested away his final remaining possession—yes, his laptop!—and he di

TEAM LEYNER TODAY!

The sensational disappearance of Mark Leyner following the expropriation of his laptop by the Federal Punitive Confiscation Tactical Division has ignited a firestorm of protest around the world! Mobs of rampaging fans have besieged U.S. embassies in London, Paris, Warsaw, Mexico City, Riyadh, and Tokyo, forcing the evacuation of terrified diplomatic personnel by troops wielding truncheons, attack dogs, tear gas, and water cannons! Shadowy underground organizations have threatened the lives of American political leaders and Fortune 500 CEOs and—in clandestine radio broadcasts—urged children to subliminally indoctrinate their parents by murmuring key passages from Leyner's texts into their ears as they sleep!

YOU can be a vital link in the Team Leyner chain of solidarity that girds the globe in Power and Bold Unity! HOW?

- The Punitive Confiscation Act is an outrageous attempt by the federal government to squash Team Leyner, persecute its leader, and drive him into the arms of his enemies. *Write to your congressmen and senators demanding that they immediately repeal this misbegotten legislation that exists solely to impede a historic visionary in the fulfillment of his destiny.*

- Book sales are crucial. If Mark Leyner is alive—and we must assume that an individual who, as a toddler, honed himself into a ferocious, cunning, and pitiless animal will survive whatever befalls him—he's certainly monitoring the best-seller lists and *Publishers Weekly. There's no better way to register your support for Leyner and everything he stands for than by urging—and, if necessary, coercing—your family, friends, and co-workers to bulk-order* Et Tu, Babe *from their local bookstores.*

Remember, when you purchase a copy of this inspirational volume, 100 percent of the proceeds go to funding important Team Leyner projects such as:

- The production of large-print, Braille, and pop-up editions of Leyner's work

- The construction of the Buffway, a 600-mile-long suspension bridge in the form of Leyner's outstretched body that will span the Arabian Sea linking Ras al Hadd, Oman, to Karachi, Pakistan

- The development of the World Institute of Advanced Science, a research facility in Palermo, Sicily, that will reevaluate evolution from the Big Bang through the Cretaceous demise of the dinosaurs to the present moment as one continuous teleological process leading inevitably to the birth of Mark Leyner and to the propagation of his genetic lineage through sexual intercourse and auxiliary methods including "mole seeding"

Call 1-800-T-LEYNER today for an exhortatory message from Mark Leyner to his fans recorded in the heroic hours before his disappearance! Stay on the line to record your personal words of support for the man whom food-and-lifestyle authority Martha Stewart has described as having "the face of an angel and the glands of a god!"

Seed the Minds of
the World with
Team Leyner Thought!

Help disseminate the incendiary words of this visionary warrior by ordering additional copies of Mark Leyner's majestic master works for your family, friends and co-workers.

Available at
Your Local Bookstore